The Sky Looked The Same

Marissa Dike

PAGE PUBLISHING, INC.
Conneaut Lake, PA

First originally published by Page Publishing 2021

ISBN 978-1-6624-5325-0 (pbk)
ISBN 978-1-6624-5326-7 (digital)

Printed in the United States of America

*To Erin, Marie, Olivia, and Trey—for seeing
all the things I couldn't see anymore.
To Jacob, for believing in me when I don't believe in myself.*

To anyone who might read this in the future,

Today, I asked for a pen and a notebook.

I always wanted to be a writer when I grew up, and growing up is coming to me sooner than I expected. I'm constantly starting stories but never finishing them. I don't know if I'll finish this one. Right now, I just feel like I need to write everything down because in a hundred years, when I'm long gone and I have no idea what the world will look like, I want at least one person to know what it was like—what it was *really* like—to live right now. Forget what your history books tell you. Forget what the government tells you. If, by some miracle, this book makes it into your hands someday, I want you to know that I am absolutely 100 percent telling the truth.

Okay? Good.

Today's date is November 14, 2088. We aren't supposed to know that, but I know a bunch of us have kept track anyway. The official date is the seventy-sixth day of the eleventh year. Today, I am sixteen, but I don't know how old I will be by tomorrow. I have a mom that hates me and a dad that barely tolerates me. I don't blame them. I've been a pain in their asses since the day I was born.

I'm sitting in my holding room, waiting for them to bring me my dinner even though I probably won't eat much tonight. I don't get nervous very often, but tonight, I'm nervous. It's not a welcome feeling, and I hate that I can't control it.

There were five of us in my group: three boys and two girls. We found each other five years ago at the beginning of sixth grade. We were the only kids that didn't fit in anywhere else, so we clung to each other. Jorge was the oldest. He had gotten held back a grade; I can't remember which one. He had six younger brothers and sisters, and he had to take care of them most of the time. His dad had run off years earlier. His mom worked eighty-plus hours a week most weeks. She loved her kids, and she loved their friends. She made sure we were all fed even if it meant she had to skip a few meals herself. She was so much more like a mom to me than my own mom was. I'll always love her for that.

Matty was tall, gangly, quiet, and the most unassuming kid I've ever met, who somehow grew ten inches and gained at least one hundred pounds in the span of two years. By the end of eighth grade, he could barely cram his body into the crappy metal desks at school. He looked menacing and could easily take out anyone who wanted to mess with us. But to his friends, he was a gentle soul, a brother, someone who would give you his undying devotion. He was so easy to love. I don't think I'll write anymore about him because I get choked up just thinking about him, and I don't need any more emotions controlling me right now.

Juniper was my best friend. She had a bunch of sisters, and they were all named after trees: Willow, Maple, Sycamore, and there was one more but I can't remember what her name was. Her parents were barely parents at all. They were more like cool older siblings that let us smoke pot with them whenever we wanted. Juniper once confessed to me, while we were super high and no one else was around, that her dad had molested her when she was little, and she was worried that he would do the same thing to her little sisters. She made me swear not to tell anyone, and I didn't. I guess it really doesn't matter now.

Then there was Elliot. My sweet, sweet Elliot. From the first day we met, we were inseparable. I remember seeing him for the first time, and I just couldn't keep my eyes off him. He had dark brown skin, he had dozens of braids cascading down his back, and his eyes were the most stunning shade of green. When we were fourteen, we kissed for the first time, and the first thing I said was, "What took you so long?" We bonded over being the only child in both of our families and having apathetic parents. He held my hand gently while I softly cried and told him I was pregnant, and he responded by telling me that he would be there with me, from doctor's appointments and looking through potential adoptive parents' profiles to holding my hair while I threw up in the school bathroom. I miscarried four weeks later. He asked me how I felt, and I took a deep breath and told him the truth: I felt relieved. We couldn't be parents. I was too afraid to get an abortion, and I was even more afraid of giving birth. So it was for the best, all of it, and we made sure to be way more careful from then on.

And then, finally, there was me. Mia. I'm not beautiful even though Elliot told me he thought I was the most beautiful girl in the world. I'm not smart even though my teachers all told me that I could be a great student if I applied myself. I'm not particularly good at anything, truthfully, other than lying my way out of trouble. My parents had me after years and years of trying, and from the moment I was born, I was a disappointment. I cried constantly. I didn't talk much. I couldn't read. I threw temper tantrums. And their solution was to ignore me. I don't blame them for how I ended up, but sometimes, I wonder what I could have been if they had paid attention to me even just a little bit.

Someone just knocked on the door. My dinner's here: some sort of microwaved green vegetable, instant mashed potatoes, and a dry, gray pork chop. I know I should try to eat it, even just a part of it, because who knows when they'll feed me next. Sentencing days are notoriously unpredictable from what I've heard.

I'll take a break and come back after dinner.

—Mia

I've introduced myself. Now I'm going to tell you why I'm here.

The short version is I made a mistake. A really bad mistake. And now my friends are dead and my parents won't see me and everyone else probably hates me, and I don't blame them at all. Whatever happens next, you should know that I deserve it, all of it, whatever's coming.

It all happened seven days ago. But even before it happened, things in our group had started to change.

Jorge had come to school with bruises on his face. He told us he'd been in a fight, but he wouldn't tell us who he'd fought with even after Matty swore he would kill whoever it was.

The bruises never healed. They just moved around. Whenever one would start to fade, another one would show up right next to it. It's no big deal, he'd said. He had been getting into some fights, he'd said. He didn't want us to know anything else.

We all knew better though. We knew that, whatever was happening to Jorge, we couldn't leave him to fight his battles alone. So one day, Elliot and I skipped our last-period class so that we could hang around the outside of the school and wait for Jorge to come out so that we could follow him home. We walked so far behind Jorge that we could barely see him, slowly and quietly, hoping he wouldn't notice us. He seemed completely paranoid, looking around his shoulder with every turn. It was almost impossible for us to stay hidden, but we somehow managed it.

What I saw next is still hard to write. It's all so damn unfair, and anytime I think about it, my mind goes blank and my fists clench, and I end up punching my wall and getting bloody knuckles.

Out of nowhere, three giant guys came up to Jorge. He froze. I could tell even from far away that he recognized them. They exchanged words, first by talking then by shouting. And before I knew it, two of them grabbed Jorge's arms and wrenched them behind his back while the third one punched him over and over until he was barely conscious, and then they just left him lying on the ground and walked off. Jorge stayed on the ground for a few moments, and he was gasping and coughing, and he spit up a little bit of blood onto the ground. But then, he cautiously stood up, brushed himself off, and continued on his way home as if nothing had happened.

Elliot and I just stayed frozen in place hiding behind a dumpster the whole time. Whether it was out of fear or shock or numbness, I'm not sure. All we could do was look at each other, each of us waiting for the other one to say something. I remember the flies and the smell of rotting garbage swirling above our heads and Elliot looking lost and afraid.

This was a problem that would take all of us to solve. I sent a message to Matty and Juniper, telling them to meet us at Jorge's house. Then Elliot and I stood up and began walking. We didn't say a word to each other the entire way.

Jorge opened the door for us. I'll never forget his face. He looked so much worse up close, with his purple lips and swollen eyes and broken nose. One of his front teeth was chipped. Blood was dried and crusted around his ears. I hugged him. I didn't know what else to do. I felt him start to sob on my shoulder, and all I could do was whisper, "What is happening to you?"

After we got Jorge to his room and helped him clean himself up, we got the full story.

It had all started at a party he'd gone to a few weekends prior. It was mostly for the popular kids only, but Jorge had gotten an invitation because he was a friend of a friend of the party's host. While he was there, he met a girl. He didn't really think much of her at first, just that she was pretty and seemed to still be somewhat sober.

I should probably mention here that Jorge is—I mean *was*—gay. He wasn't officially "out," I guess; only his mom and our little group knew about it. So he never went to parties with the intention of picking up anyone, much less girls. But this girl was persistent. Jorge only had a couple of beers in him. Nothing too heavy. The girl was following him around and not being very subtle about it. They ended up in a part of the house that was almost empty. He could tell she was into him. He was trying to figure out how to let her down easy when out of nowhere she just started kissing him. He kissed her back, just for a second, because he didn't know what else to do.

Then she started getting aggressive, shoving him against the wall, reaching for his pants, groping him. He tried to push her off him, but she wouldn't stop. She just kept pushing up against him. He didn't want to hurt her. She was small. He kept saying no over and over. She wouldn't listen. He had no choice. He grabbed both of her arms, lifted her out of his way, and ran.

"Guys, I swear to God, I didn't mean to hurt her," he said. "You believe me, right?"

Both Elliot and I nodded emphatically. Of course, we believed him. I asked him what happened next.

The girl ran off crying. Jorge felt bad. He thought that would be the end of it.

But the girl had a boyfriend. And she had bruises on her arms from where Jorge had grabbed her. And she told her boyfriend that Jorge had come on to her and had gotten violent when she rejected him. The boyfriend had friends. And they found Jorge and beat the shit out of him. They did it again after school that Monday and again the next day and the next and the next.

"And, guys," he whispered in terror, "I don't think they're ever going to stop."

Elliot and I looked at each other, silently agreeing. "They'll stop. Tomorrow," I said with determination. Elliot nodded. "We'll all make sure of that."

Jorge sat up and shook his head violently. "No, no, no. This is why I didn't tell you, guys. I don't want you getting hurt too."

"There's five of us and only three of them," Elliot replied. "And I'll bring a knife, too, just in case. They won't even touch us before we get them to the ground."

I grabbed Elliot's hand and squeezed it in solidarity. He was right: there were five of us, and all of us were fighters. People always underestimated Juniper and me since we were girls, but we could easily hang with the boys in a fight. Neither of us were particularly small, especially Juniper, who was nearly six feet tall and had the broadest shoulders I had ever seen on a girl. We both had short, violent tempers and had been in fights since grade school, a habit that made Juniper's peace-loving parents shake their heads in disappointment and then look the other way while my parents just locked me in my room and refused to let me leave other than to go to school. It was hardly a punishment; I just snuck out of my room when they weren't paying attention.

When Matty and Juniper showed up, we made our plans. We would all walk to school together the next day, keeping Jorge in the middle of us to make sure he stayed safe. We would meet up after school and hide behind the dumpster, just like Elliot and I had done, and we would wait for them.

I was the last one to get there. Matty, Juniper, Elliot, and Jorge were all waiting for me just outside the fence. We all had the wide-eyed stares of simultaneous fear and excitement.

"You got the knife?" Matty asked Elliot.

Elliot answered by flashing a glimpse of metal sticking out of the inside pocket of his jacket, and we all smiled. But before he could close his jacket back up, I saw something that the others had failed to notice.

There was another piece of metal, concealed well but still visible if you were really looking for it. It was small, it was just barely sticking out of the waistband of his jeans, and it had an unmistakable outline.

A gun.

Heart pounding, I looked into Elliot's eyes with bewilderment, and I knew that he knew I had seen it. We could have entire conversations with just our eyes. *Don't you dare say a word,* his eyes were saying. And from that point on, I understood that something terrible was going to happen.

We continued to wait behind the dumpster and spy on everyone who passed us. Some of them gave us weird looks. Most didn't even bother looking in our direction. Then Jorge grabbed my hand. He was shaking. "That's one of them," he whispered.

A boy was walking by himself, slowly and deliberately, like he was looking for someone. Elliot pulled his knife. The rest of us stayed completely still and silent, every joint in our bodies wound up and ready to spring.

The boy spotted us without much effort. He strolled up casually and looked down at us without saying a word. He had a beautiful face. I wanted to destroy it.

"So you brought reinforcements, huh, Martinez?" he said. "You even brought some girls along. Do you get off on that, Martinez? Do you get off on seeing girls get all bruised up? You're sick, man. You know that?"

Juniper stood up and stepped forward, her face inches from his. They were almost the same height. "We asked to come," Juniper said quietly. She never raised her voice. She didn't need to. Her physical presence was menacing enough. "We're here to make sure Jorge stays safe."

The boy just started laughing. "So you get girls to fight your battles for you, Martinez?" he asked. "How do you live with yourself, you cowardly piece of—"

He couldn't finish that thought because Juniper suddenly and silently grabbed him, flipped him over, and slammed him to the ground on his back. The rest of us gathered around him, looking down at his gasping face. "Will you leave us alone?" Juniper asked calmly. "Or does this need to be settled some other way?"

He rolled over onto his side and let out a few coughs. He was covered in dirt but didn't look injured. Juniper hadn't wanted to hurt him. If she had wanted to hurt him, he would have been hurt. He glared at her, eyes filled with hatred.

"If you want to settle this," he said coolly, "you'll meet us here tonight." He pointed to the alleyway behind the dumpster. "Nine o'clock." He stood up and spat in Juniper's face. She didn't even flinch. None of us did. We just stood there, watching as he turned and walked away. Elliot was still stroking the blade of his knife with his thumb.

"Nine o'clock," I echoed, slowly panning over the faces of my friends.

I didn't go home that night. It's sort of strange to think about, but I haven't been home since that morning. I spent the rest of the day with Elliot, just wandering, getting food, fooling around in his car—all the stuff we usually did, and all the stuff we'd never do again.

The moon was out and the crickets were chirping by the time Matty, Jorge, and Juniper made it back to the alley where Elliot and I were waiting. The five of us sat, rarely breaking the silence, which was something we did often. We were drawn to each other like magnets, and it was enough for us to just soak in our combined energies. I may have even dozed off on Elliot's shoulder because I don't really remember the boys showing up. I just opened my eyes, and there they were, six of them this time. I felt a little nervous then. As strong as we were, we were still outnumbered.

One of them stepped forward with his hands up. "We should talk," he said, and his voice was surprisingly not aggressive. He was the biggest of all of them, and the rest of the group seemed to be following his lead.

Elliot stepped forward to meet him. "Yea, I think we should too," he replied.

The moonlight through the tree branches made all kinds of patterns across their bodies and faces. We all stood there just staring each other down for a while, none of us wanting to be the one to break the silence. Finally, Elliot spoke up. "Look, we just want you to leave our friend alone," he said, but he didn't sound very sure of himself. The boys all looked at each other, then back at us.

"Why should we do that?" one of them asked.

That's when I began to change. I don't know how else to describe it. I just felt my body morph into something else, something reckless and dangerous and bad. I reached into Elliot's waistband and pulled out the gun before he could stop me. "Because we're armed," I answered, shaking with adrenaline. "And we don't want things to get ugly."

The six of them gasped collectively and stepped back. "Shit! Where the hell did you get that?" one of them shouted.

Elliot gently reached over to me and lowered the hand that was pointing the gun at them. I honestly don't even remember raising it. "It doesn't matter where we got it," he answered. "What matters is we're all alone out here. We could kill you all in seconds, bury your bodies somewhere, and no one would ever find you."

I eyed him curiously. It was a giant threat, and there was no way we could carry it out. But it didn't matter. The boys were scared enough. "All right, man," said the big guy, still with his hands up. "All right. Understood." And then they turned and started to walk away.

That should have been it. We should have all gone home after that. But I let them all down.

The boy with the beautiful face.

If he had said it just a little softer or said it when they had gotten further away or just not said it at all, then I wouldn't be sitting here. I keep telling myself that even though I know it isn't really true. Like I said, I was turning into someone else. I felt evil welling up inside me, and I knew it wouldn't take much for it to burst out.

If only I hadn't heard it.

If only.

Because as the boys were walking away, the beautiful one whispered something, and it was that something that cut me open and released the devil. It burned my ears, it bored into my skull, it crawled down into the pit of my stomach and made me want to vomit.

"Stupid nigger," he said.

And I looked at my Elliot, my beautiful Elliot, with his beautiful brown skin shining in the moonlight and his beautiful black braids and his beautiful green eyes that held my whole world inside of them.

And I snapped.

I can't tell you what happened next. I can't tell you because I honestly don't know. This is what everyone says happened.

I still had the gun in my hand. I began shooting, and I shot until the gun was empty. They had knives. They rushed toward us. We clashed together like two armies, shooting and stabbing and punching. I ended up on the ground. I remember feeling pain in my right arm and feeling blood trickle down my forehead into my eyes. I remember there were lots of shouts and then sudden silence. I remember fading in and out of consciousness before I was finally hauled to my feet, bandaged, carried, and shoved into a vehicle.

When all was said and done, I had killed three of them. The other three managed to get away with minor injuries, but not before taking care of the five of us.

Matty was dead.

Jorge was dead.

Juniper was dead.

Elliot was dead.

Everyone thought I was dead.

I *wish* I were dead.

Somebody just came in to take my dinner tray away. They never give me much notice when they come: just three knocks on the door, a jingling of keys, and then the huge metal door scraping over the cement floor and slamming against the wall. It's ironic. I'm alone in my cell almost all the time, and I still feel like I never get any privacy.

After I was brought here, the first thing I can remember is being forced into a metal chair that was fused to the floor. My handcuffs were still on—too tightly because they were leaving red marks all across my wrists—and a chain was wrapped around my waist, and I had chains and cuffs around my ankles. Somebody hooked me to a table and walked out of the room, and then it was just me and concrete and metal and chains, all wrapped up together like some sort of freakish symbiote. *Symbiote: an organism in a partnership with another such that each profits from their being together.*

I actually really love biology. My teacher, Mr. Fuller, had wanted to be a surgeon. He went to school for it and everything. But something happened to him, something really terrible. He never said anything about it, but the rumor was he had an affair with a man, and his wife found out about it and left him. I don't know why something like that would make you not want to be a surgeon anymore. At any rate, he became the biology teacher at my school, and he's been there for almost thirty years. He never got married again, not to a woman or a man. He talked about sex in the most blunt, clinical sort of way possible. It made everyone else cringe, but I liked it. Once, he showed us a picture of a human brain scan during an orgasm. It was so beautiful.

"During orgasm, the brain releases several chemicals, such as dopamine, oxytocin, and endorphins. We can see the effects of these chemicals on certain parts of the brain in this image here."

I stayed after class and shyly asked Mr. Fuller if he had any more pictures of the brain I could see. I spent my lunch hour with him, just scrolling through photo after photo on his computer screen.

"This is your brain when you sleep. This is your brain when you hear music. This is your brain when you are depressed. This is your brain when you are aroused."

The next time I had sex with Elliot, I thought about my brain lighting up red and orange and purple, and I wished that I could open up my head and see it in real life.

I sat alone for a while before two people walked in. One was a man. He looked barely older than me and carried a big metal brief-case. The other was a woman with dark hair pulled back so tightly that her eyebrows were permanently raised in a look of surprise. She pulled up a chair and sat next to me—my lawyer. The man sat across from me and gave me a friendly smile as if I were his date meeting him for coffee and not a person who had just killed three people.

"Hello, Mia," he greeted me. He pulled out a recording device out of the case, set it on the table between us, and pressed a button. "I'm going to be asking you a few questions about the events that occurred last night. I'll be recording our conversation. I just want you to tell me, to the best of your ability and memory, in your own words. What happened?"

I could hear a soft *whirring* sound from the ancient-looking ceiling fan above me that was spinning way too fast. "I want this to feel casual," he said. "Just a casual conversation. Don't be nervous. Just tell me what happened." He leaned forward slightly and began to speak louder and clearer. "Today is day seventy-one, year 11. I am sitting with Mia..." He paused for a moment and blushed, quickly stopping the recording. "I'm so sorry. Can you pronounce your last name for me?"

I glanced over to my lawyer, who rolled her permanently surprised eyes. *So unprofessional,* she would have been thinking. I looked back at my interrogator and suddenly felt sorry for him. I wondered how many times he had done this. I wondered if this was his first time doing it alone. "It's Einecle," I said and then added, "I always tell people to think about body parts. 'Eye-Neck-Elbow'. Except don't add the 'bow' at the end."

He nodded slowly. "EYE-neck-el," he repeated carefully.

"Yeah," I said.

He smiled at me again. He was cute, with his floppy blond hair grazing his eyes and his freckled nose and his white dress shirt that was just slightly too big for him. I wished he were ugly. "I forgot to ask, can I get you anything? Coffee? Water? Tea?"

I shook my head no.

"Oh, and also my name is Detective Gavin Brenneman. I-I think I forgot to mention that."

Yes, the adorable Detective Gavin Brenneman with his floppy hair and freckles and baggy shirt had forgotten to mention that. My lawyer audibly sighed, not bothering to hide her disgust.

"It's okay," I said quickly. "Nice to meet you."

He took a deep breath and turned the recorder back on. "This is Detective Gavin Brenneman. I am sitting with Mia Einecle. We are recalling the events of the previous night, day seventy, year 11." He looked into my eyes for a few seconds before he asked his first question. "Mia, to the best of your recollection, can you tell me exactly what you did yesterday from the time you woke up to the time that you were found with the dead bodies?"

Bodies.

Juniper. Matty. Jorge. Elliot. They were just bodies now.

I felt sick. My eyes got heavy and warm. I helplessly looked at my lawyer, but she sat stone-faced, offering me nothing. Eventually I was able to choke out the story to Gavin. I never once looked up at him, and he never asked me to. When I was finished, he handed me a tissue. I hadn't even noticed that I'd been crying. He had been furiously scribbling stuff down the whole time and kept scribbling after I was done, and the scratching of his pen and the whirring of the ceiling fan were the only things breaking the unbearable silence. Finally, he stopped and stared at his notes, clicking his pen in and out, in and out, in and out...

"I just want to clarify one thing for the record," he finally said. He never stopped clicking his pen. I wondered if he was doing it on purpose to torture me. "You said that you were provoked by one of the boys because he had verbally abused your boyfriend. Can you tell me exactly what he said?"

I suddenly felt every muscle in my body contract all at once. The crappy breakfast sandwich they had fed me hours before threatened to come up and out of my mouth all over Gavin and his clicking pen and his scribbled notes. I felt like I couldn't breathe. I became far more aware of the handcuffs and ankle cuffs and the fact that I was chained here and I couldn't escape.

"Can-can we please stop for a second?" I begged in a whisper.

Gavin shook his head. "We're almost finished, Mia," he said dismissively. "I just need to know exactly what the boy said to you. Okay?"

No. It wasn't okay. Nothing was okay.

"He-he called Elliot the N-word," I stammered, and that's when I finally completely broke down, and with all the crap around my wrists and my waist and my ankles, I could barely reach up to wipe my eyes. Both my lawyer and Gavin remained unflinching.

"I'm sorry, Mia," Gavin replied coolly, "but I need you to repeat *exactly* what he said."

I clenched my teeth to keep from screaming. "I *did* tell you what he said."

"I need to hear the exact words. For the record."

He wasn't cute anymore. He was a monster, like the monsters who killed Elliot. He didn't need me to say the word. He *wanted* me to say it. He wanted to hear it from my mouth. He stared at me, and I swear I saw him smirking. I thought about what I would do to him if I wasn't cuffed to the table.

But I *was* cuffed to the table. Elliot was dead, and I was going nowhere. Not until I said what they told me to say. Follow the rules, keep your head down, don't make a scene. That's how I could have kept them all alive. That's how I would get out of here.

"He said 'stupid nigger,'" I said, and whatever amount of human compassion I'd still felt up to that moment left my body. I would love no one, not ever again. Humans don't deserve love.

Gavin reached over to touch my hand, but I jerked my hand away in disgust. He managed to grab it anyway. His hand felt like wet rubber. I wanted to vomit again. "Thank you, Mia. I know that was hard," he said gently with a smile. He let go of me and turned off the recorder. I felt hollow.

"Can I go now?" I asked robotically.

Gavin nodded, and two officers came in to free me from the table. They led me, or practically carried me, back to my cell. And I've been in here ever since.

—Mia

November 15, 2088
Day 77, year 11

Today, I find out what my sentence is. I've talked to my lawyer for a grand total of six minutes since I was interrogated. She had asked me how I thought I should plead, and I said that I wanted to plead guilty. I did it after all. I killed three people. Pleading innocent won't change that.

My lawyer seemed happy to hear my decision. She said that confessing what I did might lessen my sentence. I asked her what my potential sentence might be, and she hesitated a little bit. "Well," she finally answered, "given that you're a minor, you were provoked by a violent racial slur, and you have been completely honest and compliant with law enforcement thus far, I could reasonably see you getting a minimum of ten years."

I closed my eyes and let it sink in. "You really think I could get off with ten years?"

My lawyer nodded. "I do. That's the minimum sentence possible in this situation, but I do think it's very possible."

I sighed. Ten years. "What is the maximum sentence I could get?" I asked.

My lawyer frowned. "Well, by law," she answered, "you could potentially be charged for each murder individually. Ten years for each victim."

Ten years. Times three.

Thirty years.

I could be aged thirty years.

No one has been successfully aged more than twenty years. The aging experiments have resulted in thousands of deaths. Nobody cares because the experiments are being done on criminals.

I don't know much about the process. I know it takes a few weeks, and the person is supposed to be sedated the entire time. A few years ago, I heard a story about a man who had raped and murdered a four-year-old girl. He was convicted and sentenced. The doctors in charge of his aging all agreed to paralyze him without sedating him.

So he felt everything. Supposedly, it feels like burning alive from the inside out. He took it for three days until the pain finally killed him.

It's just a story. Doctors don't do things like that. Right?

It's time now. The officers are coming to get me. They'll put the shackles on my wrists, around my waist, around my ankles. They won't say a word to me or to each other. They'll lead me into the courtroom, where my mom, my dad, and all the people I've wronged will be seated, waiting to hear my fate.

Today, I am sixteen. Today.

November 15, 2088.

—Mia

November 16, 2088
Day 78, year 11

I don't have much time.

After my sentence was announced, I was immediately whisked away to a giant van and locked inside. I was surrounded by guards along the way. There was a crowd. Everyone was screaming at me. I tried to shut it all out, but my hands were shackled to my waist, and I couldn't cover my ears or shield myself from the shouts of "I hope you rot in hell!" coming from all around me.

It took half an hour to get from the courthouse to the aging facility. It was raining outside; the raindrops slammed against the tinted windows and then slithered downward like slugs leaving wet trails behind them. I took it all in, every raindrop, every branch of every tree we passed, every stoplight and pedestrian and colorful umbrella that decorated the sidewalks.

My sentencing didn't take long. I had already admitted that I had killed the boys. The only thing left for the judge to decide was how severe my punishment should be. The three boys all testified that I shot first and they were acting in self-defense. One of them cried as he spoke. Then as he was walking back to his seat, he glanced over at me and gave me the evilest grin I had ever seen. I wanted to kill him. The judge asked me if I had anything that I wanted to say to the victims' families.

Victims.

No. No, those boys were not victims.

Jorge is a victim. He never had the chance to find his soul mate, to meet a beautiful boy and fall madly in love and finally live his life without fear.

Juniper is a victim. She was pinned against the wall by the one man in the world who should have never hurt her and robbed of the chance to keep the same thing from happening to her little sisters.

Matty is a victim. He was bullied because he was too small, and then he was bullied because he was too fat. And no matter what, he stayed stoic and quiet, expressing himself through poetry and music and living for the moments when the five of us would finally find each other at the end of every day and we could forget about everyone else.

Elliot is a victim. Elliot. My beautiful Elliot. Dark brown skin and green eyes and a smile that made my knees weak. Intelligent. Motivated. Happy. And none of that mattered because the last thing that was ever said to him was "stupid nigger."

I stood. I stared each and every one of the people in the courtroom in the eye and never said a word. Then I looked back at the judge. "No, Your Honor," I whispered. "I have nothing to say." And I sat down. I kept my eyes on the table in front of me. The judge began to speak. There was an ocean in my ears that grew louder and louder with each second that passed, and the rest of my body felt like it was swimming along with it. I could only make out two things: the collective gasp from the courtroom and the words that sealed my fate.

Thirty years.

Ten for each boy that I had murdered.

And then I was lifted up involuntarily because I could barely stand and hauled away. Shoved into the van with the tinted windows. Dragged into a small room with white walls and no windows. Undressed, inspected, bathed. I hadn't had a chance to eat. I hadn't even had a chance to pee, and by the time they finally let me use the bathroom, I felt like I would burst.

That was yesterday. I haven't slept since then. I can't sleep, not with all this whiteness surrounding me.

There's a clock in here, and it's telling me that my time is coming. In just a few minutes, they will take me away to my aging room. They will pump me full of the different chemicals they use and wait. I will be asleep for at least two weeks, maybe longer, while the chemicals take effect. Footsteps down the hall, coming closer, closer...

And just like that, I'm in my room. I had expected it to be really sterile and ugly, but it's actually kind of nice. I have a comfortable bed with clean sheets. There's even a window to my left. It's stopped raining, and there aren't even any clouds in the sky anymore. The sky is blue, pure, untainted blue, and the oak tree by my window is swaying ever so slightly in the breeze. It's all so bizarrely unfitting for what's about to happen to me, like listening to a lullaby while getting every single one of your teeth ripped out one by one.

They've told me a little bit about what they're going to do to me but only because I asked. One of the aging doctors came into my room to get me hooked up to a machine that tracks my heart and my oxygen and blood pressure. He never said a word, but he seemed kind and was gentle as he was setting everything up, and it gave me the courage to ask.

"What is going to happen to me, exactly?"

The doctor had this look on his face like he didn't want to answer me, or maybe he just didn't know how to answer me. He continued prepping everything in silence for a while. "Well," he finally said, "first, we're going to put you to sleep so you won't feel a thing. Then we will pump your stomach so that it is completely empty, but don't worry, we'll make sure you're nourished and hydrated." He gestured to the IV bags he was hooking up. "We will need to remove your uterus and your ovaries first, along with most of your breast tissue, to reduce the risk of mutation and cancer. Then we will inject you with a few different chemicals and place something called an aging cylinder over you that will cover your entire body head to toe—"

"No, no, I don't—that wasn't what I meant," I stammered. "I mean, what will I be afterward?"

The doctor sat down next to me in the chair by my bed and gently placed his hand on my forearm. "A microwave oven and a conventional oven both cook food. The microwave oven is faster, much faster. But it doesn't cook food nearly as well. And that's sort of how this process works." He stood up and removed his gloves. "We are, in a way, 'microwaving' you. It won't be perfect. Some parts of your body might age differently than others, like how some bits of food get hotter than others in a microwave. But, essentially, when we are all done, you will have the body of a forty-six-year-old woman, more or less. Only instead of taking thirty years for you to 'cook,' it will only take about three weeks."

I stared down at the needles and tubes running up and down my arms. Elliot and I had microwaved a potato chip bag once. It had shriveled up to the size of a playing card, and the kitchen smelled horrible for the rest of the day. And in just a few minutes, I will be the potato chip bag in the microwave, and I will shrink and wrinkle, and I will never ever be the same again.

They're coming to put me to sleep now. It's time for me to go. I really hope I make it, but in case I don't, thank you for reading this far. I really mean it.

—Mia

December 7, 2088
Day 99, year 11

Today, I woke up.

Nobody knew if I would wake up or not, and I'm so grateful just to be able to write it down: today, I am awake.

The first thing I remember was pain. All kinds of pain. Sharp pain, aching pain, burning pain all over my insides and down my arms and legs, and my head was throbbing. "She's awake." It was a man's voice, and it sounded muffled, like it was coming from the other side of a window, but I could hear it all the same. And then I slowly opened my eyes, and I couldn't stop crying, not because I was sad, but because my eyes felt like they were on fire.

"Mia," said the voice, and again it sounded muffled. "Mia. You're awake now."

Everything was blurry, even after I blinked my eyes over and over again, and that's when I realized they had taken my glasses. I heard a mechanical buzzing sound right by my head; my bed was slowly folding up so that I was eventually sitting upright.

"Mia. How do you feel?"

It took a while for my brain to register the question, and even when it did, my tongue couldn't find the words to the answer. I just kept staring, wide-eyed, all around the room, growing more and more panicked every second. Everything was fuzzy shapes and muted colors and flat textures that didn't make any sense.

"She needs her glasses," another voice finally said, and then I felt the cheap plastic frames being shoved into my hand.

I closed my fingers around them cautiously; my hand felt so different. My knuckles were sore, my skin was dry, my nails had been cut short. I placed my glasses on my face with the hand that was mine but didn't feel like mine, and then, finally, I could see.

"Mia. How do you feel?"

It was the same question, but it came from a different person. A woman. She stood with her arms crossed and a concerned look on her face. She attempted to make eye contact, but my eyes were drawn to the window she was standing next to. The thin pane of glass separated me from the outside now, just like it had before. The oak tree with its naked autumn branches gently swayed in the wind, against a sky that was all too blue. And then the strange truth started sinking in: I was in a different body but in the same room, the same bed, looking out the same window as before.

"The sky," I croaked softly, and then I gasped because it wasn't my voice. My voice was high and sweet, not deep and crackled. I felt panic wash over me. This wasn't my voice. I began to cough, and then I couldn't stop. The woman came over to me and began helping me lean forward.

"Easy now," she whispered.

The other doctors seemed utterly disinterested. Most of them had already left the room when they saw I was awake. I felt a damp cloth placed on my forehead and a glass of water placed near my lips. "Take a drink, very slowly," she instructed, and in that moment, the lukewarm tap water was the greatest thing I had ever tasted. It was all I could do to keep from gulping it all down in seconds. She got me another glass, then another until my throat was no longer dry.

"Say it again," she said. "The sky. What about the sky?"

I don't know why it was the first thing my brain had thought to say. But that sky, the sky that was too blue for this time of year and had no clouds and made me feel like I could swim inside of it—it was the same sky that I had seen right before I went under. It was the last thing I remembered seeing.

"The sky. The sky looked the same," I choked out. And then I started crying again, not because my eyes hurt, but because the sky had stayed the same and I hadn't.

—Mia

December 11, 2088
Day 103, year 11

I've spent a few more days in the aging facility so the doctors could monitor me and make sure I was handling everything all right. Everyone was shocked at how well my body took to the procedure. Nobody in history had ever been successfully aged thirty years in one session. I am, technically, a "medical marvel." I'm probably all over the news, but I don't know for sure because they don't let you have any contact with the outside world while you're in here.

I didn't have much of a reaction when I saw my face in a mirror for the first time. It took my brain a second to register that I was staring at my own reflection and not someone else's, someone with wrinkles around her eyes and veins protruding down her neck and little white hairs sticking out everywhere. *This is my face*, I had to tell myself over and over. From now on, this was me. And so I looked for myself, in every wrinkle and crevice, and slowly I began to recognize the woman staring back at me. My eyes were still there, bloodshot and weepy, but they were still mine. My teeth were the same crooked mess as always. My hair was still a light brown frizz ball, only now it was peppered with gray and white.

I'm still me. I'm still Mia. I'm Mia, and I'm forty-six years old.

Today, I finally get to go home, but I don't really know where home will be. I know I won't be living with my parents. They want nothing to do with me. I also know that I've been set up with a job and a small apartment. I don't know what the job is or where it is or if I can even physically handle it. Every joint in my body aches constantly, and as long as I'm laying still, it isn't so bad, but when they make me get up and walk around, it's torture.

I'm going to put this away now so I can get ready to go. Everything I do takes so much longer now than it used to.

—Mia

December 12, 2088
Day 104, year 11

I'm here now.

My new apartment.

It's a studio apartment. It came furnished with a tiny bed shoved up against the far wall and a wooden table with a single chair. The floor tiles are the kind that always look dirty no matter how hard you scrub them. The bathroom is smaller than my closet was at my parents' house. This apartment doesn't have a closet, so I'm going to have to figure something out for storage. Right now, my clothes are all still in a bag on the floor. I don't have much stuff left. You don't get to keep much with you when you're aged. I have a few clothes, a toothbrush, and a comb. The rest of my stuff has probably already been thrown away. I don't think my parents want any reminders of me around them.

It wasn't that cold when I first walked in the door, but I found myself shivering anyways. "Miro, turn up the temperature three degrees," I called out. I waited. No response. Of course. This is an old apartment. Miro isn't here. *Manual-Intuitive Residence Operator.* I honestly didn't know what it stood for until about a month ago. I saw an advertisement for the new, upgraded Miro and saw it written out: "Manual-Intuitive Residence Operator." And I had one of those moments in my head where I was like "Oh, *that's* why it's called that." I wondered how many people knew what it stood for and if I was the only one dumb enough to think it was just a random name someone came up with and not an acronym, like NASA or SCUBA or LASER. The name makes sense: *manual* because you can override any of the automations and set it however you want, and *intuitive* because after a while, Miro learns your habits and behaves accordingly, sometimes with a scary amount of accuracy. Our Miro when I was growing up would automatically order a pizza for me on Thursday nights because my parents both worked late on Thursdays and would tell me to order pizza for dinner. I only had to do it a few times before Miro started doing it for me.

Does Miro still exist when you're reading this? You probably have something even better. In any case, there's no Miro in this apartment. There's no Smart Home technology anywhere at all, no VR or AR devices, nothing. I've never lived in a place like this.

There are other people who live in this building, entire families even. I was dropped off without a word in the lobby, where I was met by the ugliest man I had ever seen. He owns the building. He told me that I would be living in the smallest room in the basement floor, and in return, I would be cleaning the apartments of all the other residents and getting a small stipend for food. I have a schedule: I have to clean the apartments on the bottom floor on Mondays, Wednesdays, and Fridays and the apartments on the top floor on Tuesdays, Thursdays, and Saturdays. I could have Sundays off, he said, unless I fell behind. There are four apartments on each floor. Two are larger family units, and two are small like mine. That's eight apartments to clean. I start work tomorrow.

If you're reading this, a long time from now, know that there was a time when everything was different. I was really small when everything changed, but I remember there was a time before aging was discovered and there were these places called "prisons," and that's where you would go if you committed a crime. You would just sit in this place for ten years or twenty years or sometimes for the rest of your life. Imagine that: thousands and thousands of people just sitting in a building together for years and years and years. And then, almost overnight, it was like everything became different somehow. All these people in the prisons just disappeared. And the prisons all shut down, and they all turned into holding cells and aging labs. Because, see, it's so much cheaper to just take years away from people and then send them back out into society. You don't have to pay for their food or clothing or beds. You pay for the aging procedure and that's it. And somehow, it was decided all at once that *this* was how society would work, and age wasn't a fixed steadily moving thing anymore but instead a fluid thing that could be manipulated and changed, and humans were all going to start over from scratch. It was no longer August 31, 2077. It was year 1, day 1. I was five years old.

I would learn as I grew up that this had all been decades in the making. So much time and money and effort had been invested in the revolution. So many other things had just come to a screeching halt—technological advances, medical advances, environmental conservation—just so every bit of research could be devoted and poured into the science of artificial aging and the legislature to permit it. Cancer research was placed on the back burner while aging experiments were done on rats in labs, and none of us ever had any idea, which is a pretty shitty thing for the government to keep from the general population, if you ask me. Hopefully by the time you're reading this, cancer will have been eradicated. But as of right now, it still exists, and the doctors all tell me that in spite of their best efforts, I will most likely develop it soon and that will be the thing that kills me.

—Mia

December 13, 2088
Day 105, year 11

Today was Monday, the first day of my new job and the rest of my new life. When I knocked on the very first door, nobody answered. "Um, hi, this is the new maid," I said cautiously through the door. I knocked a second time, then a third, but still there was nothing. Nobody was home.

I froze for a second. I didn't have the door code to anyone else's apartments yet, so I couldn't go in unless someone let me in. I moved on. I knocked on the next door. Nothing. And that trend continued for the rest of the doors. Of the four doors I knocked on this morning, only one opened. A middle-aged man in nothing but his underwear stood there, staring at me, clearly not pleased to see me. He smelled like he hadn't bathed in a week, and just by seeing and smelling him, I knew I was in for a long cleaning session. I sighed.

"Hi, I'm Mia. I'm the new maid and I'm supposed to—"

"Oh, I know who the hell you are," he snapped. "Saw your face all over the news. They told us you'd be staying here." He cautiously moved away from the door, never once taking his eyes off of me. "Make it quick. I want the bathroom and kitchen cleaned and the floor vacuumed. Stay out of my room, I don't want it cleaned. Understand?"

I looked around. His apartment was a studio like mine, but part of it was sectioned off by a sheet hanging from the ceiling— his "room." I fumbled with my cheap plastic gloves and mask to cover my mouth and carried my haul of cleaning supplies into the kitchen. They were all the generic, most inexpensive kind, the kind that smelled heavily of chemicals and never sprayed consistently so there would be puddles of liquid oozing over every surface. It took about thirty minutes just to get through the mountain of dishes in the sink, and by the time I got to the bottom of the pile, the smell was so rancid that it overpowered the chemical smell and permeated the entire apartment. I did my best not to gag.

"You done in there yet? What's taking so long? I gotta go to work, and I sure as hell ain't leavin' you here by yourself."

"Yes, I'm sorry sir. I promise I'll be done soon."

My head was swimming with the mixture of chemicals and mold and what I could only assume was urine. I needed a break, so I decided to do the floors next. I found the man's vacuum and began working. It was soothing, in a way, the quiet hum of the vacuum and the mechanical motion of pulling and pushing it back and forth, back and forth, back and forth—

"WHAT ARE YOU DOING!"

My head snapped up, and my heart started pounding. The man stood there, presumably in his work uniform; he was a dock worker, apparently. His face was red. "You do the floors *last*! After everything else has already been done. That way you aren't tracking any more dirt around. Anybody with half a brain knows that! Have you never cleaned a house before?"

No, I thought. *No, I have never cleaned a house before. I'm sixteen, and my parents are rich, and they have a maid and Miro and toilets that clean themselves with the press of a button, and I shouldn't be here, I want to go home, I want to go home, I want to go home…*

"I miss Oliver," he grumbled as he grabbed his shoes. "Oliver was our housekeeper for fifteen years before I even moved in. He knew how to clean apartments, let me tell you. And he could do a whole apartment in the time it took you to do the dishes. He cleaned for us right up until the day he went to hospital. Never got out, poor guy. Stage-4 lung cancer."

My eyes began to water from the horrible chemicals-mixed-with-mold smell that was now hanging like a heavy blanket over the space. "I'm so sorry, sir," I choked out. "This is my first day. I promise I'll do better—"

He stood up and walked past me to the front door. He still smelled like he hadn't showered in a week, and I wondered briefly if he was able to smell anything at all. The smell in his apartment didn't seem to be bothering him. "You can come back later after I get home from work and finish the rest," he said, turning to face me. "I get home around 10:30 p.m. I want you to be here right then because I want to go to bed by eleven. Understand?"

I nodded. "Yes, sir. I will see you then."

It's been four hours since then. I hurried back to my apartment, and I haven't moved from my chair. I don't want to go back to that man's home. I don't know what to do about the people who never answered me. I don't know what will happen if I get fired or evicted. Will they just move me somewhere else? Will I be homeless? Will they age me again and kill me and be done with me?

I don't want to be here. I would rather be anywhere else in the world—the aging facility, my holding cell, the courtroom, the alley behind the dumpster. I remember the stars so clearly. There wasn't a cloud in the sky the night they found me lying in the grass with my dead friends all around me.

Okay. I have to stop. I can't think about the past. It's gone, all of it. This is my life now. It's a mess, but it's mine. It will get better eventually. It has to.

—Mia

December 29, 2088
Day 121, year 11

I'm sorry that it's been a few weeks since I've written anything. I've been busy getting used to my new job. I still forget which soap to use for what sometimes, and yesterday, I accidentally mixed up the laundry of apartment A and apartment F again. The Bryans live in apartment A and the Byrons live in apartment F, and I just can't seem to keep it straight in my head which is which. But other than that, I'm doing okay. The ugly owner likes me. His name is Jonah. He lives in the basement in the apartment next to mine, and he tends to leave his door open a lot. Every time I see him, he's got his giant fat body sprawled out over his couch and a beer in his hand. He always offers me one. I always say no thank you. I think maybe he feels sorry for me. He knows about me. *Everyone* knows.

The Byrons live in apartment A—no, wait. See? I did it again. Dammit.

The *Bryans* live in apartment A, one of the family units on the top floor. I've only met the wife once. She was hurrying out the door as I was walking in, and we sort of awkwardly introduced ourselves before she ran off, and now I can't remember her name. She's a waitress at some restaurant and probably has to work at least sixty hours a week to support them. The husband has an artificial leg and doesn't work. He just sits on his couch all day and watches me while I clean. He never says a word, but his eyes follow me everywhere I go, and I hate it. I always do their place first and as fast as I can.

Kyle lives in apartment B, the other family unit on the top floor, and he has it all to himself. His stepmom hates him, so his dad kicked him out when he turned eighteen. That was last year. He can't find work and has been putting everything on credit. His apartment reeks of weed. I got bold one day and asked to smoke with him after I finished cleaning his apartment, and he was surprisingly generous with his stash. I was high for a while afterward. It definitely made cleaning less terrible.

Apartments C and D are the tiny studio apartments on the top floor. The "Jennifers" live in apartment C. Both of them are named

Jennifer, but one of them spells it differently, I just can't remember how. They're lesbians in a somewhat tumultuous relationship. Sometimes, they fight right in front of me while I'm cleaning. One of the Jennifers found out that the other Jennifer cheated on her last month with their heroin dealer. Their apartment stays incredibly clean. I don't ever need to spend more than a few minutes in it at a time.

The people who live in apartment D are never home, but they always leave their door unlocked. I don't know for sure how many people live crammed in there, but I counted seven phone chargers plugged into the walls. There isn't much space to walk because there are four or five mattresses all over the floor. I don't even bother to vacuum, and they've never complained about it.

On the bottom floor, apartments E and F are the family units. Jorel lives in apartment E and only speaks Dutch. Two small girls live with him. I'm assuming they're his daughters even though they don't look much like him. They're never in school. I've only ever seen them wearing dirty nightgowns.

The Byrons (I got it right that time, hooray) live in apartment F. They just had a baby. I can't tell if it's a boy or a girl, and I'm too embarrassed to ask. All I know is that it cries whenever it isn't sleeping. I went to the apartment once, and the door was unlocked. The Byrons were gone, and they had left the baby home alone. I told Jonah about it, but nothing ever happened. The Byrons were back in their apartment the next day and didn't say anything about where they were and why.

Vandré, like André but with a V, he told me, lives in apartment G, a studio. The only furniture in there is one bed with a comically large headboard. He owns his own house but rents the apartment to use for "personal matters." I wasn't exactly interested in learning what he meant by that, but I did walk in one time, and he was naked with a woman on the bed. Neither of them seemed to care that I was there.

The nasty-smelling man I met on my very first day lives in the other bottom-floor studio, apartment H. His name is Dorian. He still hates me and complains every time I'm over. He still won't let me clean when he isn't home. He still demands that I stay out of his "room." I have no idea what he does in there. I think I'd rather not know.

And then, of course, there's the basement. It has two apartments. I live in the studio, and Jonah lives in the one with a bedroom. The laundry room is down there, too, next to the big storage room that has cleaning supplies.

So there you have it. You know where I live.

Oma, my dad's mom, used to tell me that any old place could be a home if you took the time to put a little bit of yourself in it. Her house was filled with porcelain giraffes, thousands of them. She collected them for some reason. When she died, the giraffe collection was auctioned off for over a million dollars. My dad paid off our house's mortgage with it.

I don't have any giraffes. I don't have much of anything. One of Jorel's daughters handed me a picture one day. She shyly told me she had drawn it for me. It was a picture of a witch with purple eyes and green hair and polka-dot skin. The witch had beheaded three werewolves with her broomstick.

"The red stuff is all the blood," the girl had told me.

I told her that I thought the picture was beautiful, and I hung it up on my wall with some tape. And it does make this place feel more like home somehow.

—Mia

January 1, 2089
Day 124, year 11

Today would have been New Year's Day, a holiday from the old age. I only really remember it happening once or twice, but I remember that on the night before, everyone would stay awake until midnight, until the next day began, until the New Year began. It was such a big deal to people back then, the new year arriving. It wasn't like how it is now, where you just go to your district's government hall and get your updated identification card and picture and that was it. People actually *celebrated*. There were holidays, lots of them—the New Year, Valentine's Day, Easter Sunday, Halloween, Christmas. There were others, but those are the big ones I remember because I got presents and candy on all of them.

I miss holidays. I hope that by the time you're reading this, you've gotten some holidays back. If not, give your kids some candy anyway. Tell them it's from me.

—Mia

January 5, 2089
Day 128, year 11

Secrets
A poem by Mia Einecle

We all have our secrets.
We carry them on our foreheads, behind masks
That are walls made of glass—
One perfectly placed trajectory: that's all it would take.

We'd be strangers then.
But we'd know each other well.
Well enough anyway.

Though,
We never really wanted to see what was behind the invisible walls.
We just wanted them to fall down
So we could put them back up with paper instead.
Don't sigh too loudly
Or you'll blow them away.

I was going to submit this to a poetry contest they were having at my school before everything happened, but, of course, I never got the chance to. I never showed my poems to anybody but Matty, who also secretly wrote poetry. He was the one who told me about the contest, and he begged me to submit one of my poems. I chose this one, not because I think it's my best one, but because I think it's the most honest. I know, I know, I sound so pretentious when I say things like that. Anyways, this is the only poem of mine that I remember. Maybe, I'll sit down and write some more...someday... when I feel inspired. I have to feel inspired to write poems. There I go being pretentious again. I'm sorry.

That's how I know I wouldn't have made it as a real writer. Real writers don't rely on random bursts of inspiration. Real writers can just write even when nothing is in them. A local author visited my

English class last year to give a guest lecture, and someone asked her about her process. She just shrugged and said, "I write. Every day, I write. I spend an hour every morning and two hours each afternoon just writing, writing, writing. Some days, I write more, if there's something in particular that I need to get out. But most days, I stick to my schedule. You have to fight through the writer's block. Just write. Whatever it is. Even if it's bad. Write it down."

And everyone looked awestruck and motivated, and I just sat there knowing I could never do it. Blank screens. Blank pages. I just don't have it in me to turn them into something remarkable at any given moment. That's just the truth of it. Writers can write and painters can paint and actors can act and singers can sing and swimmers can swim every second of every day.

So, hey, if you're actually reading this, thank you. You're making my impossible, ridiculous dream come true.

—Mia

January 9, 2089
Day 132, year 11

I am 100 percent certain that my mother never loved me.

I think that maybe my father could have loved me, but he loved her more, and so the greatest feeling he could summon for me was total indifference.

They had tried for years to have a baby. My mom finally got pregnant and had me when she was thirty after who-knows-how-much money in medical procedures, shots, medications, and visits to the clinic. From the moment that I was conceived to the moment that I was born, I was monitored constantly, my mother's uterus under practically twenty-four-hour surveillance. Anything that she thought was at all slightly irregular sent her rushing to the hospital, only for them to tell her that everything was fine, that I was perfectly healthy, that I was growing at the proper rate and moving like I was supposed to. And then I was born.

I don't know what I did wrong other than come out a purplish, writhing, screaming thing like all of us do. I've only heard the story once, and I honestly only ever needed to hear it once. My dad got really, *really* drunk one night, and he finally told me the story of my birth.

My mom was exhausted and delirious from all the drugs. The nurses took me away and cleaned me up, like they always do with newborns. My dad had a weak stomach and opted to stand in the corner of the room as far away from his blood-soaked new daughter as possible. It couldn't have taken more than a few minutes, but I shrieked the whole time, those high-pitched baby shrieks that feel like they're gonna burst your eardrums open. And apparently, my mom yelled out from her bed, "Can you *please* just shut her up? My god, suffocate her if you have to! Just *enough* with all the damn screaming!"

The nurses and my dad all froze, and my dad swears that even I stopped crying for a moment. I don't know if my mom really said that. I don't know if any of the story is true or if it's all a misremembered, exaggerated mess. But finally, supposedly, one of the nurses turned to my dad and said, "It's totally normal. She's in shock and delirium from all she's been through. I guarantee you she won't remember any of this by tomorrow." And then somebody put me in my mother's arms for the very first time, and that's when I started crying again. And my mom just stared down at me, expressionless, and then turned her head back up to look at my dad, and she looked him straight in the eyes and said, "This is it?"

She had been expecting more, much more, though I'm not sure exactly what it was. She expected more my whole life. I didn't learn how to walk or how to use the toilet or how to speak soon enough. I didn't want to be a ballerina like she was, and I sat on the floor with a scowl during the expensive dance classes she forced me to attend. I stayed perfectly silent while she screamed at me until I eventually learned the strength of my own voice. My father sat passively by as he observed us verbally abusing each other, day in and day out, until one day my mother slapped me. I remember that day. I was twelve years old. She stood in front of me, arms crossed across her pathetic excuse for breasts as I lounged lazily on the couch messaging with Juniper and Matty and Jorge and Elliot. She ordered me to get up. She accused me of doing nothing with my life. She said that when she was my age, she had already traveled around the world with her ballet company. She said I was lazy. She said I was fat; I was 115 pounds. She said no boy would ever love me. I was disgusting. I was undesirable. I was worthless.

None of these things were anything new. She had said them hundreds of times before, and I had screamed and cried and looked desperately to my dad to say something, *anything*. But I felt different that day. I stood up, already as tall as she was. I stared into her eyes. They were nothing, just dead orbs, windows into a soul incapable of love.

"Get the hell away from me," I said coolly. And then I felt it. The hand rushing to meet my face, the sting afterward, the cut under my eye where her diamond ring had connected with my skin. I didn't cry. I barely flinched. I just sat back down on the couch, and she silently left the room.

She rarely yelled at me after that. We resorted to cold, ugly silence, only saying the bare minimum to each other whenever we absolutely had to. By the time I was sixteen, she was a stranger. I lived in Juniper's basement, on Matty's couch, in Elliot's bed. My own room was as unfamiliar to me as a hotel room.

My father got more and more pathetic the older I got. He would beg me to come home and have dinner with the family. I would ask him if he thought Mom wanted me there. He would say that he was sure she would. And I would tell him that he was a coward and I hated him for it.

So, reader, I guess you can be the judge. Maybe I was born evil, and my mother sensed it. Maybe I was a disobedient asshole even as a toddler. Maybe kids should never yell at their parents, no matter what. Whatever, I'm tired. I'm tired of thinking about it and questioning it and wishing it maybe could have been even a little bit better. I'm just writing it all down here, and then I will never think about it again.

—Mia

January 20, 2089
Day 143, year 11

I met someone today. His name is Joel. I met him while I was sitting on a bench waiting for the shuttle to take me back home from the hospital. Ever since I was aged, I have to go back to the hospital every two weeks to make sure there's nothing wrong with me. The tests are the same every time. They take blood and urine samples, they check my skin, hair, and teeth, and they x-ray my chest to make sure my lungs and heart are okay. I asked one of the doctors if it was normal to have to get checked every two weeks after getting aged. She said most people only get two or three checkups during the first few months, but I have to get checked up more often because no one else has ever been aged thirty years at once and no one knows what terrible, terrible things could happen to me. I don't mind. It gives me an excuse to leave my apartment building and watch the city go by from the shuttle window. Nobody ever pays attention to me in the city even though I was all over the news after the murders. City people forget things quickly.

The shuttle was running behind today, and while I was waiting for it, somebody sat down next to me. A deep male voice let out a loud, contented sigh and said, "Nice weather today, huh?"

My body immediately tensed up. A stranger was talking to me. I hate talking to strangers. I didn't answer him. We just sat in awkward silence for what felt like forever, and then the shuttle showed up, and I got on as fast as I could without looking behind me.

I sat in the seat farthest to the back and leaned my head against the window while I waited for my stomach to drop from the sudden acceleration. The stranger who had spoken to me on the bench took a seat near the front, but not before we made accidental eye contact, and I quickly looked away in embarrassment. He was short, pale, and he had this awkward way of walking with his feet turned in. I turned my head back frontward as he took his seat and got a good look at the back of his head. He had a bald spot that somehow didn't look like it belonged there.

The shuttle lurched forward, and that's when I finally began to settle in and relax. Everything began to pass by my eyes with incredible speed. Colors and objects blurred together in an ever-changing mural. The low hum of the shuttle's engine was familiar and soothing. My eyelids began to grow heavy, and my head slowly drooped forward. I was always exhausted after the hospital visits. But just as I was about to drift off, I felt something stirring next to me, and I jolted awake.

"I'm Joel."

A pale face was now inches from mine. My head felt dizzy. My voice was trapped in my throat. I didn't know Joel, and I didn't really want to.

"I'm not a creep, I swear," he said, and he backed away and held his hands up to convince me. "You just-you look really familiar, and I know I've met you somewhere, but I can't remember where and it's bugging me."

I kept my eyes down and shook my head. "I don't know you. I'm sorry," I whispered, hoping he would get up and leave. He didn't.

"I've definitely seen you somewhere though," he insisted. "Do you live nearby, or—?"

"No," I cut him off. And finally, my hostility worked.

"Okay. I'm sorry. I didn't mean to bug you." He got up and smiled at me. "Have a nice day, ma'am."

Ma'am. He called me ma'am.

But I'm not a "ma'am." I'm Mia. I'm just Mia, and I'm alone, and I'm scared, and I'm too young to be so old. And I started to cry, and as he was walking away, I blurted it all out. "I'm Mia Einecle. I was convicted of three counts of murder and was aged thirty years. You probably saw me on the news or something. That's why you recognize me."

He turned and looked straight into my eyes, and for just a moment, I felt fear. Would he be disgusted? Would he be angry? Would he be violent? But no. He wasn't any of those things. He just looked...*sorry*. For *me*. He quickly sat back down next to me.

"So how old are you?" he asked casually, not at all concerned that I'd just told him I'd murdered three people.

I swallowed the lump that had formed in my throat. "I'm forty—"

"No." He cut me off and shook his head. "I mean, how old are you, really?"

My heart started beating fast because, of course, you aren't supposed to ever acknowledge your birth age after you get aged. Maybe, the laws are different for you reading this in the future. Today, even bringing it up in casual conversation is dangerous. If someone overhears and cares enough to report it, it's an automatic additional year of aging. But this guy wasn't out to get me. I don't know how I knew that, but I did. His eyes somehow just told me that he could be trusted. And I had spent so much time trying to deny my real age, trying to forget about it like you're supposed to do. But you can't forget it. You always know the truth deep down. And I wanted to just say it out loud, to let the truth escape my body and live and breathe in the real world.

"I'm sixteen," I whispered and looked down at my bony, wrinkled hands in shame.

Joel took a sharp breath inward. "Oh, shit," he mumbled. And he put his arm around my shoulder without asking, and I let him, and we sat just like that, two practical strangers on a shuttle speeding forward to nowhere that really mattered.

Eventually, he turned to look back at me. "I'm nineteen," he said, and I knew from his gray hairs and the slight wrinkles around his eyes that he wasn't really nineteen in the eyes of the government.

"Really?" I shifted in my seat. "What did you do?"

Joel shrugged. "Lots of stuff," he said. "Drugs, assault, shoplifting. I stole a car once. None of it was so bad in the grand scheme of things. But the time, it adds up after a while." He started doing math on his fingers. "I think I'm up to fifteen, no, sixteen years now," he said. "I'm supposed to say I'm thirty-five." Then his eyes grew dark with defiance. "But I'm not thirty-five. All the experimental shit they do to us, it doesn't change a damn thing. Remember that."

The shuttle suddenly jolted to a stop. Joel stood up. "It was nice to meet you, Mia Einecle. I really mean that." He walked off and left me alone but not before gently pressing a piece of paper into my hand. It was his contact number.

—Mia

January 28, 2089
Day 151, year 11

Something happened in Jorel's apartment today, and I'm still a little shaken up by it. I thought that maybe if I write about it, I won't feel so upset.

When I knocked on the door, one of the girls opened it. Jorel was in the shower, so I couldn't clean the bathroom. I got started in the kitchen. His kitchen isn't quite as disgusting as some of the other kitchens here, but it's always filled with dirty cookware. I'm not sure what he cooks in there. Whatever it is, it always leaves behind a greasy residue on everything.

I had almost finished in the kitchen when Vera, the older girl, approached me. I told her hello. She didn't say it back. She just stood there, staring at me while I dried the pots and pans with a hand towel. When I had finished, she finally spoke.

"I can make Olma disappear," she said with a smile.

I peered into the living area, where the younger girl was sitting with her back to us, quietly playing with a doll that was missing an eye. "How do you make Olma disappear?" I asked.

"It's easy!" Vera cried. "Watch!"

And slowly, she began to sneak toward her sister without making a sound. That was when I first noticed the small blanket she was hiding behind her back. *She was probably going to throw it over Olma's head*, I thought. It was hardly a disappearing trick, but whatever, I could muster up some fake enthusiasm for a kid.

That's not what happened though. What happened was Vera suddenly wrapped the blanket around Olma's neck and began pulling as hard as she could. Olma began letting out silent screams, desperately grasping at the blanket, but Vera was bigger and stronger and had caught Olma by surprise.

I stood paralyzed in disbelief, just for a moment. Then I leapt toward the girls. "Vera! No!" I screamed and tried to pull her away. But her grip tightened. She was strong. Stronger than me. I didn't have the strength to physically overcome a little kid anymore. So I ran to the bathroom door.

"Jorel! Help me!" I screamed and banged on the door. In the corner of my eye, I could see Olma's face turning purple, and she was no longer struggling.

Jorel came out with nothing but a towel around his waist. When he saw what was happening, he shouted something at Vera that I couldn't understand, and she immediately let go. Olma lay motionless on the ground.

I rushed toward Jorel's phone, ready to call in the emergency, but he yanked me away. "No!" he shouted firmly, and then more quietly a second time, "No." And then he looked at both girls in silence. I felt like my own heartbeat was the loudest thing in the room.

Then Olma's tiny body began spasming and coughing uncontrollably. Vera stomped her foot and screamed something at Jorel in Dutch, and he screamed back and slapped her across the face, and Olma continued to choke on the floor. I knelt by her head and stroked her hair and reassured her with a shaky voice that she was going to be okay. When she finally stopped coughing, she slowly sat up and blinked a few times. Then she took a deep breath and continued to play with her doll like nothing had happened.

Jorel, seemingly satisfied with how the situation had turned out, returned to his shower. Vera sat huddled in a corner sobbing in anger. I packed up my cleaning supplies in a daze with shaking hands. But before I left, I turned back to Vera. "Vera, why? Why would you do that?" I cried.

She looked at me, her face wrenched in an angry scowl. "I wanted the lights to come!" she wailed at me. Then, suddenly, she jumped up off of the floor, shoved me outside, and slammed the door in my face.

She wanted the lights to come.

The ambulance lights.

She had done this before, I realized: choking Olma, calling the emergency number, squealing with glee as the ambulance arrived flashing its lights. While the medics worked on her sister, she would simply stare out the window at the lights, and when it was all over, Jorel would be left with an ambulance bill that he certainly couldn't afford. Maybe it had happened once, maybe it had happened half a dozen times. In any case, she wasn't at all deterred from trying it again.

I am feeling a little better now after writing it all down. But I can't help but wonder if, in time, Vera will be the next person to be aged thirty years.

—Mia

January 29, 2089
Day 152, year 11

It's Juniper's birthday today.

It's day 152 of the eleventh year, but really, it's January 29. And Juniper was born on January 29. She would be seventeen.

She wouldn't *really* be seventeen, of course. We all turn a year older on the same day, day 1 of the new year. But I remember when we all used to have our own birthdays, our own day to celebrate. I've forgotten mine, but I never forgot Juniper's.

On her fifteenth birthday, the five of us celebrated by skipping school, stealing Elliot's mom's car, and driving to the ocean. Matty brought beer. I brought weed. We drank and smoked till sunset then ran into the ocean in our underwear. In my whole life, I've never been so cold and so happy.

After Elliot dropped everyone else off at their houses; he took me back to his. I shivered the entire way. I shivered as he carried me up the stairs to his room. We had sex for the very first time, and when it was over, I finally stopped shivering. I fell asleep in his arms with his braids cascading around my shoulders and down my breasts. Every now and then, he would gently wake me with soft kisses across my neck and ears.

I miss them all so much. Sometimes, it all hurts so bad that it sucks the air out of my lungs, and I feel like someone is stepping on my heart and I'm scared it will burst open like a grape that's been squashed. That's how I feel today.

I knocked on Jonah's door this morning and told him I was sick and couldn't work today. He told me he understood and to get some rest. I don't know if he meant it. I don't care. I got back in bed, and I've been drifting in and out of consciousness, and when I'm awake, I cry, and when I'm asleep, I eventually wake up crying.

Maybe, this will be the last January 29 I'll be alive for. Deep down, I hope it is.

—Mia

February 2, 2089
Day 156, year 11

I saw Mom today for the first time since the sentencing.

I was at the market to pick up a few things for dinner, and she was in the produce section squeezing lemons. She looked right at me, but she didn't recognize me. We've never looked the slightest bit alike. I look exactly like my dad—light brown curly hair, blue eyes, square German-looking facial features. My mom is small, delicate, dark-haired, and brown-eyed. Even now that we're both forty-six, we still look nothing alike. Her face is still youthful, her hair has yet to turn gray, her eyes have no signs of crow's feet.

Anyways, I went up to her. I went right up to her, in the middle of the produce section, and I said, "Hi, Mom."

It startled her, and she stood really still for three or four seconds before it finally clicked in her head. "Mia," she said stiffly. She put her bag of lemons in her cart and began to study my face. "You look well," she decided.

I've never felt anything even close to love toward my mother. At our best, the only feelings we could summon for each other were tolerance and cold detachment. But in that moment, for some reason, my heart ached for her to love me.

"It's good to see you. I mean that," I said, and I tried to sound as sincere as possible. She looked confused for a moment, then just turned away and began reaching for more fruit. That's when I noticed it.

On a woman as tiny as my mother, it was impossible not to notice her stomach. Round and firm, like the melons she was grabbing.

"You're...pregnant," I stammered in disbelief.

She spun around and wrapped her jacket tightly around herself as if I had just walked in on her naked. I continued to stare intensely at the bulge she was unsuccessfully trying to conceal beneath her jacket. At her age, with her medical history, the odds had been astronomical. But there it was, right before my eyes.

A miracle.

"Mom, I'm so happy for you," I said, and my eyes began to get misty.

She noticed, and it softened her for a moment. Slowly, she unwrapped her arms from around her waist and looked down, beaming like only a mother would do. "We found out right after you," she said softly. She put a hand on her belly and smiled. "He's our little miracle."

He?

It was a boy?

My entire childhood had been spent asking for a brother, asking and asking and asking until one day my mom burst into tears and my dad screamed at me for upsetting her. I never asked again after that, but the wish had never gone away. Not even now. And before I could stop myself, I said in utter disbelief, "I-I can't believe I finally have a brother."

The softness in Mom's face quickly turned cold again. "He is *not* your brother," she replied. Her voice trembled, and her face was red from anger. "You are no longer a part of this family. You forfeited that right a long time ago. You will never meet him, you will never see him, and he will never know you even exist. Do you understand?"

"Mom, I—"

"No! I am not your mom. I'm his mom. *His* mom! *He* is my baby. Not you."

Tears streamed silently down my face across every new wrinkle and blemish. I wanted to hang onto them, whatever her last words to me would be. No matter what they were.

Her whole body was shaking now. "God…God gave us a new start," she whispered. "We prayed for it, and he gave it to us. I can start over. I can finally have the family I always wanted…"

Her voice trailed off. I was still crying, right there in the middle of the supermarket. I didn't give a damn what anyone thought. And then finally, she said them. Her last words to me.

"Please, stay away from us. If you care about our family at all, you won't contact us. You won't search for us. You won't ever speak to us again." And then she grabbed her purse and took off toward the exit, leaving me behind with her cart full of lemons.

—Mia

February 7, 2089
Day 161, year 11

Do you remember Joel, the man I met on the shuttle a few weeks ago?

Tonight, I finally got up the courage to call him.

I had to give up my phone after my conviction. When I was released, they gave me a new one. It's not actually "new," it's the model from like five years ago. It doesn't feel great on my wrist. I forgot how heavy old phones used to be. And the earpiece is big, and it always falls out when I move my head around too much. But it works, and it's better than nothing.

"Call Joel," I said to my wrist with a shaky voice. I couldn't decide if I wanted him to answer or not. Then...

"Hello?" His hologram popped up in front of me. He was outdoors; I couldn't tell where.

"Hi, Joel, um, this is—"

"Miiiaaaa." His grainy hologram smiled at me, and he had sort of an inebriated look on his face. "Of course, I remember you. From the shuttle. How are you?"

I took a deep breath. "I'm...fine. How are you?"

He glanced around at his surroundings. "Well, currently I'm walking out of a bar, and I'm headed straight to another bar. Alone. Isn't that the most pathetic thing you've ever heard of, Mia? Doesn't that just make you wanna cry?" He laughed and hiccupped and laughed some more.

I felt a whole lot of the embarrassment you feel when someone is being a complete moron in front of you and has absolutely no self-awareness. The Germans have a word for it: *Fremdschämen*. In case you didn't know. The Germans have a word for just about everything.

"Joel," I asked, "are you sure you're okay?"

"Mia," he replied, and this time, he sounded somewhat sober, or at least serious. "I do this almost every night of my life. It's a great way to cope. I promise."

"This doesn't sound like coping to me."

"Well, it is," he snapped. Then, gently, "Why don't you join me, kid?"

Kid.

The first time we spoke he called me "ma'am." Now, he was calling me "kid." I couldn't help but smile. "Where?"

"Rohn's Street Bar. Know where that is?"

"Yes."

"Meet me there in ten." He hung up without saying goodbye.

When I got there, I spotted Joel immediately. He had two beers in front of him. One was already half gone, and the other one he slid toward me. I finished it in three large gulps and set the glass down without saying a word. His eyes were wide.

"Daaaaaamn," he slurred. "You want another?"

I nodded, smiling. Inhibition was draining from my body as quickly as I had drained the beer from my glass. Before I knew it, three more empty glasses were sitting in front of me, and my head was swimming, but in a good way. We probably looked ridiculous to everyone else—middle-aged and drunk as twenty-one-year-old sorority girls—but we didn't give a damn. He kissed me every now and then, sometimes on the ear, sometimes on the neck, sometimes on the lips, and I never pushed him away. It just felt good to be wanted.

"You wanna stay with me tonight?" he whispered at one point, his breath sending the scent of alcohol swirling around my head.

That's when a different part of my brain kicked in suddenly. *No, you don't want to stay with him. You barely know him. You're both drunk. Just say good night.* And yet somehow, I ended up in an unfamiliar apartment, littered with empty beer bottles and dirty clothes and the lingering smell of microwaved dinners that had permanently made a home in the couch cushions.

But here's the amazing part. Nothing happened. He just sloppily shoved a pile of stuff off the bed, fluffed the pillows, and invited me to lay down. "You take the bed, I'll take the couch," he said.

My brain, thick with alcohol, didn't think I heard him right. "Wh-what?"

"Come on, Mia. You think I'd get you drunk, bring you back to my place just so I could have my way with you?" He grinned and shook his head. "Nah. I'll see you again. And again and again. There'll be plenty of chances for, you know, everything. Not tonight though." He stripped down to his boxers and threw the clothes on the floor then collapsed face down on his couch. Within seconds, he was asleep.

But I couldn't sleep.

I just laid there in Joel's bed, hour after hour. I glanced down at my phone: 5:37 a.m. I could hear Joel snoring on the couch and wondered what was going on in my head. As reckless as I used to be before I was aged, I would never in a million years stay in a strange man's apartment by myself. In fact, I rarely went anywhere by myself. Juniper or Elliot or both of them were always with me, hanging on my side like a handbag. And just like a handbag, you sort of forget it's there until you don't have it anymore.

That's when I started thinking about all of them. I missed them. Elliot. Juniper. Matty.

But I forgot who was left.

Oh my god.

I looked down at my phone again.

5:40.

5:41.

I couldn't remember him. I couldn't remember my best friend's name.

It's the aging. My brain. They ruined my brain. They warned me this could happen.

I stared wide-eyed up at the ceiling, and it felt like it was getting closer to my face and the walls were getting closer to the bed and the sheets felt like they were going to strangle me. I had to get out. I had to get home to my journal and frantically flip through the pages until I saw his name in writing.

Jorge.

I forgot him.

How is that even possible? We had been woven together like string; there was no way to tell where one of us started and the other one ended. Am I going to wake up and not remember my own name someday?

Anyhow, that's the story of how I went home with I man I met on a shuttle and then left while he was sleeping when I couldn't remember the name of a different man.

—Mia

February 8, 2089
Day 162, year 11

I haven't stopped thinking about Jorge. I'm afraid that if I stop thinking about him, I'll forget him forever. I'm going to write down everything I can possibly think of about him, all the things I loved about him, and so if I do end up forgetting, I can come back to my notebook and remember.

Jorge was lanky, and sometimes, when he wasn't getting enough to eat, he looked emaciated. He never brought food to school or went through the lunch line. He didn't want us to make a big deal about it, but I started packing two lunches every day and let my mom silently judge me for bringing so much food. I told Jorge to never mention it to anyone. It would be our secret. He cried. So did I. And then neither of us ever acknowledged it again.

He was a beautiful boy. His face was smooth and brown, and his eyes were black pools; you could see your reflection in them if you were really looking. He came out to the four of us when he was fourteen, but we all knew deep down already. I saw the way he looked at certain boys in our class, the ones with the perfect hair and perfect smiles and good grades, the ones that were way too good for any of us. I can't remember the name of his first real crush—some generic boy name that started with a T, like Trevor or Travis or Timothy. Jorge always just referred to him as T.

T had a girlfriend. He had a girlfriend when he confessed his feelings for Jorge. He had a girlfriend when they kissed for the very first time. He had a girlfriend when he told Jorge that nothing could ever happen between the two of them and no one could ever find out. He had a girlfriend when Jorge laid with his head on my lap, alternating between heart-wrenching sobs and trembling silence. T probably still has that girlfriend. She probably doesn't know anything about Jorge because Jorge was a good person, and he never outed T to anyone.

Maybe, T will marry her and they'll have a bunch of kids. Maybe, after forty years, he'll finally leave her for an unassuming biologist like Mr. Fuller.

I don't think Jorge ever truly fell for anyone else after T. I think he was afraid to. In any case, he loved us more than he loved anyone else. I can't explain in words what it meant to be loved by Jorge. It was an honor not given to many. To be loved by Jorge was to be a part of his family. He loved intensely and relentlessly. There were times it would overwhelm me because I didn't know if I was capable of feeling love so completely the way he did. But it didn't matter because he never asked for it in return. He wanted to protect his family from everything horrible in the world. He always had that clean boy smell, not like that overpowering cologne smell but like soap and laundry detergent. He took pride in his appearance and somehow figured out how to look great with hardly any money for clothes. He would play with my hair while we smoked on the beach. He gave the greatest, most comfortable hugs. He always managed to stay happy, and it wasn't fake happiness. He just genuinely loved life and himself and all of us.

I miss you so much, Jorge. I honestly don't know if you were a person or an angel or maybe you were a little of both. I do know that I didn't deserve you. And I'm sorry. I'm so, so sorry. I promise I will never forget you again.

—Mia

February 12, 2089
Day 166, year 11

Kyle let me smoke with him again today, and I found myself telling him things that I probably shouldn't have. I told him about my conviction. I told him about my friends. I told him my real age. He was too stoned to react to any of it. Maybe that's why it was so easy to just let it all spill out. It was like writing but out loud.

"Do you think they'll ever find a way to make us age backward?" he finally asked after a long, heavy silence.

"No. Why would they?" I asked.

He sat up and started rolling another joint. "I don't know. What if they make a mistake? What if they age someone too much? What if the person they aged was innocent and they don't find out until later? They have to be able to undo it, right?" He stuck the joint in his mouth and lit it. The heat in his apartment was unbearable. A few sweaty strands of hair had fallen out of my ponytail and were dripping sweat down my neck. I took a long drag and exhaled slowly.

"Honestly? I don't think they give a shit about any of us," I answered. And we spent the rest of the afternoon smoking in silence.

I could be wrong. Maybe there *is* a way to reverse it all. It doesn't matter to me. I'd never be eligible for it. If you killed someone back in the old days, you could be put to death yourself, and that definitely couldn't be reversed. That's what I've been given: a death sentence. Every time I go back to the facility for a checkup, all the nurses tell me I'm doing as well as everyone had expected, and they give me a sad look. And even though they won't just come out and tell me, I know that no matter how many checkups I have and pills I take and needles they stick in me, I'm not going to last another year.

I hope things are different for you now, whenever you're reading this. I hope everything has gone back to the way it was. My dad told me that once when he was a teenager, he got arrested for drinking and driving. This was back when some people still had to be in control of their cars, like you had to steer it with your own hands and look out the window and make sure you didn't drive into anything, so it was really dangerous to drive drunk. And he spent a few nights in jail, and he said he learned his lesson and never drank and drove again. That, to me, sounds simple. You sit somewhere and you learn your lesson and you move on with your life without having to see a doctor every two weeks and spending every morning throwing up from all the medications you have to take and dyeing your hair to keep all the grays from showing.

I remember at the beginning of year 11, I was so excited to get my sixteen-year-old ID card. Jorge had already had his for a year, and it looked so official and important with his contact number printed in gold numbers and his picture on a glossy background and the words YEAR TEN/MARTINEZ, JORGE MARTIN/SIXTEEN YEARS in big letters underneath it.

My sixteen-year-old ID card lasted less than one hundred days. My new one features my current picture. It still says YEAR ELEVEN/ EINECLE, MIA ELIZABETH. Then next to it, my age: FORTY-SIX YEARS. I do my best to never look at my card. I hand it face down to anyone who asks for it. I swipe it as quickly as possible whenever I pay for something and put it away immediately. I'm dreading August 31. Year 12, day one. The day I'll get my year-12 card and turn forty-seven and have a picture taken of my exponentially aging face.

Before I left Kyle's apartment, he handed me a generous bag of weed. "I doubt you get paid enough for all the work you do here," he said to me. I didn't even have time to say thank you before he pushed me out and closed the door. I'm not going to smoke it today or tomorrow or the next day. I'm saving it for the inevitable day where I'm really, *really* going to need it.

—Mia

February 17, 2089
Day 171, year 11

Joel finally found me.

I was waiting for the shuttle to take me home from the hospital, and he just walked up to me and smiled at me like we were old friends. "Well, hello there, Mia," he chirped and took a seat next to me. "I wasn't sure I'd ever see you again after the other night. After you bailed on me."

I felt my face flush. I was embarrassed. Or maybe Joel was embarrassed for me. Or maybe I was embarrassed for Joel for being embarrassed for me. I don't think the Germans have a word for that. "What are you doing here?" I asked.

He shrugged. "You told me you have to go to the aging lab every two weeks for a checkup. I just did the math," he said.

"So you were looking for me on purpose?"

"I mean yeah. You left without saying goodbye, and I just wanted to make sure you were okay."

"That's creepy, Joel." But then I softened a bit. "It's also kind of sweet."

Joel scooted closer to me. He smelled like cheap cologne and breath mints. "So come on, Mia," he said. "Tell me why you left. I thought I was being a perfect gentleman." He put his arm around my shoulders, and I felt my back stiffen.

"It wasn't you," I answered. "It had nothing to do with you. I had a lot on my mind, and I needed to get home to be alone for a bit."

He looked at me skeptically. "You sure?" he asked.

I nodded. My skin tingled underneath the thin sweater where his hand was resting.

He took a deep breath and said, "I know it's not like we have any sort of history or anything, but if you need to, you can always talk to me. I consider you a friend. You know?"

My chest felt heavy. All my friends were dead, and I didn't want any new ones. "Thanks for the offer," I said. The shuttle was approaching in the distance, and I stood up.

He stood with me. "Don't be a stranger. Please, Mia."

"I'll call you, Joel. How's that?"

"When?"

"Whenever I feel like it."

He grinned, and I blushed. "Fair enough," he said. And then he walked away.

I'm home now, and I'm exhausted. They had to take more blood than usual so that they could run a few more tests. I've been slipping in and out of consciousness all afternoon. It feels like the conversation with Joel happened weeks ago and not this morning. And even though I really meant it when I wrote that I didn't want any new friends, I think I need one right now. I guess we'll just have to see what happens.

—Mia

February 19, 2089
Day 173, year 11

So today, I learned that I've underestimated the catharsis of small talk. I always thought it was beneath me somehow, like every word out of my mouth needed to be this ocean of profundity or else it wasn't worth saying. But when your brain starts slowing down and thoughts flow through it like sticky syrup instead of fountain water, you can't always wait to speak until the really exceptional things show up. Sometimes, you just have to say whatever is on your mind and let the syrup river take you wherever it's going to go.

I called Joel today. He looked surprised, like he hadn't expected that I would actually call him. "I'd like to see you," I blurted out. He was sitting on his couch in his bathrobe. It was 2:00 p.m.

"Okay," he said. "Where?"

"Same bar as last time. I'll pay."

He gave me a weak smile. "Meet me in an hour."

The bar was empty, like most bars are at three in the afternoon. I sat in the back corner with two beers ready. He was late. Super late. And when he finally did show up, he looked terrible. He hadn't shaved or showered, and his clothes were dirty.

Unlike Joel, I actually made an effort to look nice today. I put on my least baggy sweater and thick makeup all over my face and a careful bun in my hair. I felt stupid and angry. Joel didn't comment on my appearance at all.

"Thanks for the beer," he said as he sat down. He gulped down half of it without making eye contact.

"Um. You're welcome."

I watched as his eyes darted around the room, taking in the tacky decor, the stained menus, the mannerisms of the bored bartender absorbed with her fingernails. He was utterly disinterested in me, and I hate to admit how much it bothered me.

His eyes finally made it back around to me. "So why did you want to see me?" he asked.

I clenched my beer, letting the condensation from the glass drip down all over my clawlike hand. "Honestly, I don't know. I just wanted to apologize for running out on you the other night."

A slow, lazy smile spread across his face. "No worries. All is forgiven," he replied. He leaned back in his chair and knocked back the rest of his beer.

"You want another?" was all I could manage to say.

He held up his hand and shook his head enthusiastically. "Absolutely not," he said. "You've been more than generous."

I could tell that every second he was spending with me was a second he would rather be spending doing absolutely anything else. I wanted to scream at him. I opened my mouth ready to spit out venom, but, no, that wouldn't do. Not in a bar. I swallowed it back.

"You're acting strange," I said matter-of-factly.

He said nothing, just stared straight at me with an intensity that could have made the walls around us crack. Then he stood up. "I'm sorry. I shouldn't have come to see you today," he said, and for the first time, I saw the slightest trace of emotion flash across his face. "I had a bad night. I wasn't planning on leaving my apartment today. This was a bad idea, bad idea, Joel, a really bad idea..." and then he just sort of trailed off, quietly rambling to himself until I finally stood up and grabbed him by the shoulders. Our eyes met again, and he stopped.

"You don't have to tell me anything," I said firmly. "You don't have to say a damn word. Just sit with me. Please. I'm tired of being alone all the time."

It was the first time I had admitted it out loud. I didn't say it in any pathetic sort of way. I didn't cry or plead. It was just a statement of fact. I was lonely. And I needed a friend.

And Joel just shrugged and said, "Okay. I guess I'll have another then."

Minutes later, he had his second beer in hand, and that's when I found myself making small talk, which until today was something I didn't think I was capable of doing. Every conversation I ever had with Elliot and Jorge and Matty and Juniper had always seemed so deep, so *meaningful*, and now I'm starting to think that maybe we were all trying too hard to seem profound all the time, and it would have been nice to, every now and then, just talk about things that ultimately meant nothing so we could focus all our energy on how beautiful it felt just to *be* together. And if I didn't fully appreciate the rejuvenation of small talk, then I certainly do now after Joel said what he said next.

"I have cancer."

No sequiturs. No emotion. Nothing to prepare me for it at all. I racked my brain for something to say but came up empty-handed.

"Liver cancer. I've had it for a few years now, pretty much ever since I started getting aged. It goes into remission and then comes back, goes, and comes again. They're using this experimental treatment now to see if that will make it go away for good. Sometimes, I'm in a lot of pain. Like last night. I was in a lot of pain, so I couldn't sleep. That's why I'm not myself." He shrugged. "So there. Now you know."

Still, I said nothing. What should I have said? "That's terrible." "I'm so sorry." "Everything happens for a reason." "You'll get better, I'm sure you will."

No. Sometimes, it's okay to make small talk. And sometimes, it's even better not to say anything at all.

And after a few seconds of silence, Joel went back to talking about whatever it was we had been talking about, and I slowly felt myself relax. It was what we both needed. We didn't need sympathy. We didn't need answers. We didn't need consolation. We just needed another person to drink with.

Three hours later, we finally stood up, both of us feeling content to part ways. He kissed me on the cheek and invited me to come over tomorrow night. I said yes.

"By the way," he said as he began to walk away, "you look beautiful today. Don't think I didn't notice." And then he winked at me and flashed a smile, and I quickly turned to walk away before he could see me blush.

—Mia

February 20, 2089
Day 174, year 11

Smaller Oceans
A poem by Matthew Evander Hollenbeck

Eventually,
the ocean will dissipate into the sky
and carry itself a thousand miles away,
where it will find me,
and sprinkle itself down to where I am sitting,
alone,
with pieces of the ocean pooling at my feet,
making smaller oceans.

There was this notebook that Matty carried with him all the time. It was blue and filled to the brim with his poetry. Sometimes, he brought it out around us. Sometimes he didn't. But anytime he brought it out, he would always read from it, just to us. And when he read from it, he wasn't Matty the giant, Matty the loner, Matty the kid always getting into fights and mouthing off to teachers. He was transformed into his true self, the self that only we ever saw. He could say a million things in a single phrase. He would keep us captivated for hours. Sometimes, we would all fall asleep in his room listening to the sound of his voice.

I don't know what happened to that notebook. Matty's things ended up scattered throughout all of us for safekeeping: his clothes were in Elliot's locker, his VR headset was under Jorge's bed, his computer sat on the floor of my bedroom closet. He never really had much of a place in the world and neither did any of his things. But he always kept that notebook with him. It would have almost certainly been on his body when he died. There was no one to give it to. He had no family other than an older brother that he'd never met and had never wanted anything to do with him. He hopped around foster homes until he turned sixteen and decided to make a go of it on his own. He got a job making pizzas on the weekends and moved in with a drug addict named Wayne. It kills me to think of that notebook in a dumpster somewhere, moldy and rotting on top of a pile of sticky plastic bottles and dirty diapers. All those poems, Matty's entire life immortalized in prose, just wasting away.

I hope that you turned into the ocean, Matty. And I hope that the next time it rains, it will be you sprinkling yourself down all over me.

—Mia

February 24, 2089
Day 178, year 11

Well, today I finally met the people who live in apartment D.

I went over there to clean. I opened the door that is always left unlocked. Today, instead of finding an empty room with mattresses on the floor, I found six people all sitting with their backs against the wall and VR headsets on their faces. I almost jumped, it freaked me out so bad.

"I'm so sorry," I managed to blurt out. "I'm just going to clean in here real quick and then I'll get out." I was met with silence.

There was a thick sense of dread in that room. Bad energy pulsed through the walls down to the floor and up into my feet. I felt paralyzed. I wasn't sure what was going on, but I knew I needed to do my job and get the hell out as fast as possible. Apartment D never takes me very long to clean. The kitchen is empty, other than the occasional food residue left behind on the counter. The bathroom is small enough to finish in less than ten minutes. I don't bother with the floors since there isn't really floor space. Dirty towels and trash bags come with me. It usually takes me fifteen minutes to do the whole place. Today, it took me less than five. I grabbed my bag and began rolling my cart out the door. But before I could close it behind me, a voice called out from the inside.

"You're Mia, aren't you?"

I felt the hairs on the back of my neck stand up. I peered back inside the apartment. Not a single one of them had moved. I didn't even know which one of them had talked to me. "Did you need something else?" I asked timidly. "I'd be happy to get it for you."

Slowly, one of them pulled the VR mask off their face and looked at me. Their short hair, makeup, and completely bland clothing made it impossible to determine their gender. They held out their hand toward me; every finger had a ring on it.

"Come here," they said. Their voice was hypnotizing and honey sweet.

Before I knew it, I found myself stepping across the mattresses and taking the hand offered to me.

"Sit down. I want to show you something."

I haven't been in VR since I lived with my parents. My own VR mask broke when I hid it in my backpack after my parents grounded me from it and it accidentally fell out while I was taking something out of my backpack. It made a heartbreaking crunching sound as it hit the tile. The entire class looked at me with wide eyes. If it had been any other teacher in any other class, I would have been in automatic detention; personal VR devices weren't allowed on school property. But it was biology, and Mr. Fuller just gave me a sympathetic look and went back to explaining that night's homework assignment.

I always gave my old VR masks to Jorge since his mom couldn't afford one and my parents always bought the latest models the second they came out. Jorge was my lab partner that semester, and he reached over and squeezed my hand under the table. I looked at him, and even with the bruises covering his face, I could see exactly what he was thinking: he was going to try to give me my old mask back, but I would refuse it. My parents could afford to buy me a new one. I would grovel, and they would yell, but at the end of the day, my dad was too proud to let his only child go without the latest technology, and he would buy me whatever I wanted.

Of course, that never happened because a few days later, I was chained to a table across from Detective Gavin.

"Sit down," the voice said again. "Don't be scared."

The rest of them laughed, eyes still hidden behind their headsets. I somehow ended up on the floor, and the next thing I knew, a VR mask was being placed over my face. It was the newest one, newer than the one I used to have. It weighed almost nothing. I wondered how long I'd have to save up my money to be able to afford one. I don't think I'll live long enough to find out.

The screen slowly turned from black to light blue. A high-pitched sound played so quietly that I wasn't sure if I was really hearing it or not. Then, suddenly, an image appeared. Someone was sitting motionless in a chair in the center of a completely white room. A white bag covered their head, and a white blanket was draped over their otherwise naked body. They didn't appear to be tied down, but they didn't seem to be able to move; they had been paralyzed by something.

"What is this?" I asked, barely above a whisper.

No one answered. Minutes went by, and nothing happened. I was about to take the mask off and leave when suddenly another person appeared in front of me: a tall man dressed in white from head to toe with his head completely shaved and covered in white paint. The tall man approached the chair slowly and silently, concealing something underneath his white robe. The high-pitched noise grew louder.

"What is this?" I demanded again, more firmly this time, but still I got no answer.

What happened next is really hard to write because it happened so fast that I can't be sure I even saw what I think I saw. In one swift motion, the tall man pulled a sword out from beneath his robe, and the next thing I knew, the head of the person in the chair was on the floor, still in the white bag, only now it was turning red. Everything was turning red, bright red, blood red, splatters on the floor, splatters on the wall, splatters on the tall man's painted face running down, down, down—

I screamed and yanked the mask off my face. The others took their masks off slowly. Six pairs of eyes were glued to me. Their faces were blank except for the slightest sinister smiles. I tried to stand, but I was shaking too violently.

"Mia," one of them finally said. "Mia. It's okay. You're one of us."

I screamed again and sobbed into my hands. "I want nothing to do with you! You hear me? You can all burn in hell!"

But they all started saying it. "Mia, it's okay. Mia, You're one of us. Mia, don't be afraid." Two of them held me still while a third forced a warm, tasteless liquid down my throat. I tried to resist.

"Please, Mia. This will make you feel better."

They were right. In just minutes, I felt a numb calm wash over me like an ocean wave. My sobs turned into silent, warm tears streaming down my face.

"Mia. You are *one* of us. Do you understand?"

I shook my head. Of course, I didn't understand. These people were insane.

"I was aged too, Mia," said the impossibly sweet voice that had invited me in. "Ten years. I murdered the man who killed my father."

I took a closer look. Their short hair was speckled with gray, their makeup settled into the crevices all over their face, their baggy clothing hid what I could only assume was a shriveled, wrinkled body.

Then, one by one, other voices began to speak.

"Five years. I assaulted my husband when I found out he was cheating on me."

"Three years. Stole from my neighbor."

"Seven years. My cop brother was doing illegal drugs and pinned it all on me when he got caught."

"You are one of us, Mia."

The drink was making me dizzy, whatever it was, and I closed my eyes and leaned back against the wall for support. The voices continued, flowing in and out of one another as though they all belonged to one person.

"Boris Patel. Fifty-one years old. One of the many scientists responsible for the development of artificial aging. Today, today, he faced his judgment. And how fortunate for you that you were here to witness it!"

Red. Bright red. Blood red. Splatters on the floor. Splatters on the wall. Running down, running down, running down.

And I was there to witness it.

I got home and immediately threw up.

My head is starting to clear up now. I'm not sure what to think, but I do know one thing: I'm getting pretty damn tired of all my neighbors.

—Mia

February 25, 2089
Day 181, year 11

I woke up at dawn this morning in a cold sweat. I had dreamed about Boris Patel. I had dreamed about the white room. And in the dream, I was the person holding the sword.

At what point do people deserve to die? I killed three people, and I'm still here.

Juniper's parents didn't believe that anyone deserved to die. Not ever. They didn't believe in war. They didn't believe in capital punishment. They didn't believe in violence of any kind. The girls weren't even allowed to compete in sports because it fostered the concept of superiority, and that was what ultimately led to war.

That's why I didn't believe Juniper at first when she told me that her father had raped her.

We had been lying on our backs in the grass looking up at the stars, both of us nursing a good high. "Don't joke about stuff like that, man," I had said angrily after she told me. "That's messed up."

"I'm not joking," Juniper had replied matter-of-factly.

I rolled over on my side and stared her down. She didn't move a muscle. "I know your dad would never do that," I said. "I know he wouldn't."

Juniper just smiled and closed her eyes. "I was ten."

"Ju, this isn't funny."

"He came into my room one night. We smoked together."

"Shut up."

She rolled over and grabbed me by the shoulders. "It's not what you think," she said, eyes wide. "He kissed me. On the face. Like all over my face. Then he told me how beautiful I was and how proud he was to be my dad. And he told me that our souls were connected. They would always be connected. And he wanted to show me. And he told me that it was just between the two of us."

I started to cry then. I couldn't say anything except "I'm sorry" over and over. She wasn't listening. "He just kept telling me 'It's beautiful. It's so beautiful' the entire time," she said. "I was so high I don't even remember what it felt like. I was bleeding like crazy afterward though."

I turned away from her and puked onto the grass.

"It's going to happen to my sisters," she said, and that was the only time she sounded even a little bit emotional. "I know it will."

I just realized that I'm crying while I'm writing this; a teardrop just landed on the page.

Juniper's dad deserves to die.

Everyone is saying that it's going to snow today, and I don't mean the normal frost sprinkle we always get this time of year. It's going to actually really snow for the first time in thirty-five years. A few flakes have already started to fall. I've never seen snow in real life before. I've only seen pictures from when the world was colder.

I'm going to go back to sleep now, and maybe when I wake up, everything will be white.

—Mia

March 4, 2089
Day 186, year 11

We've all been snowed in for almost a week now. Just when the temperature starts climbing high enough to melt the snow, another fresh layer falls. I couldn't get to the hospital for my appointment yesterday because they still can't figure out how to get the shuttles to run. Centuries of technological advances in humanity, and a little bit of frozen water throws everything off.

It hasn't snowed like this since before I was born. Back when we were allowed to keep our own copies of photos, Dad showed me pictures of himself and his brother as kids playing in the snow. They had stacked up two big balls of snow, jammed two sticks onto either side, and called it a snowman. He told me there hadn't been a snowfall on earth since that day, other than the snow in the North and South Poles. But those don't count, he'd said, because nobody actually lives there.

My eyes had gotten wide as he spoke. I'd had so many questions. How did people live in the snow? Wouldn't you freeze to death? Wouldn't all the plants and animals die? Dad assured me that snow used to be just another type of weather, like rain or sunshine, and most people got by just fine as long as they had enough warm things to wear, and the city governments knew how to keep the roads safe.

Does it snow, reader? Whenever you read this, I hope you have snow. It's so beautiful and sad. It shuts everything down and makes everything quiet. A lot of people have frozen to death. Is it terrible that I don't care?

I haven't been outside yet. I've been content to simply look out my window with a warm drink in my hand while I'm wrapped in every sweater and blanket that I own. Jonah let me have the entire week off since all my cleaning supplies are frozen in their bottles, and he's convinced that if I try to heat them up, I'll cause a chemical reaction and the building will explode.

Six hundred years ago, people thought the earth was flat. Four hundred years ago, people thought that witches were real. Less than one hundred years ago, people didn't believe that the world actually was getting any warmer and they did nothing to try to stop it from happening. And now here we all are, sitting in a world that's round, where it doesn't snow, and witchcraft is nothing more than really advanced technology. What will we learn a hundred years from now? What will we have been wrong about?

—Mia

March 10, 2089
Day 192, year 11

The Winter Followed Me
A poem by Mia Einecle

One morning,
I stepped out of my house into a wide outdoors,
and the winter followed me.
And she's been following me ever since.

When I ask her why,
she never answers,
only shakes her head and smiles.
She holds a secret only snowflakes know.

I'll run and hide somewhere she won't go.
I close my eyes; I count to ten,
but then, her icy grasp is around my wrist.
And I know she's found me.
And she carves frozen streams into my hands,
and I let her.

I spin around, but she's already gone.
She's hiding from me; she thinks it's a game.
So I try to sneak up on her.
But she jumps out of her skin,
and leaves bloody footprints in the snow.

    This one isn't so bad. It's a lot better than the "Secrets" one that I had planned on submitting to the contest at school. If I could go back in time, I would bring this new poem with me and show it to Matty. He would love it. Then I would show Elliot. Elliot would pretend to love it but only because he loved me. What he would really be thinking is "Why would you write a poem about snow?" And he wouldn't know that I could read his mind, and I would answer angrily, "It isn't about snow." And he would ask, "Well what is it about then?" And I would answer with all the pretentiousness in the world, "If I have to tell you, then you don't get it." And then I would tell him that I had come from the future and I had seen snow with my own eyes, and he would just stare me down with adorable skepticism. But fifteen weeks later, when it actually did snow, he would be mystified and afraid. I would tell him that it's all right, I've chosen him to be my time-traveling partner, and we would jump around space and time, hand in hand, for the rest of our lives.

I'd be happy with less than that though. So much less. I don't need to hear his voice. I don't need him to put his arms around me. I don't need him to acknowledge me at all.

I just wish, so, so badly, that he could see the snow.

—Mia

March 13, 2089
Day 195, year 11

I went outside today. The snow has melted down a lot, and I can walk in it without my ankles getting buried.

I don't know how much bare, untampered-with nature is left in the world. Some people say the world is fine, some people say the world is ending, and most people are somewhere in the middle and don't really give a shit either way. But today, I felt like I saw nature for the first time.

Snow defiantly covered building tops, cars, satellite towers, all the things that humans have devoted life and money and sweat and blood to build. And one simple act of nature has made everything just stop.

The body count continues to rise. The current news reports are all saying that the various snowfalls across the nation have resulted in over one hundred thousand deaths. Some people don't have access to the medication that they need. Emergency services have been having difficulty getting to people on time. No one has been able to communicate with one another, and transportation has stopped. Everything is pure chaos. And yet there I stood, in the middle of an icy street, and I had never felt more at peace.

I'm sure in a few more days, almost everything will be up and running again. Humanity has a way of bouncing back like that: identifying problems, finding solutions, making sure history doesn't repeat itself. Except that history repeats itself all the time. If your dad's an alcoholic, then you'll be an alcoholic. If your mom is crazy, then you'll be crazy. If one persecuted person rises above his persecution, then the world will find someone else to hate. Countries collapse in on themselves, wars start and end, the rich get richer and the poor get poorer.

I miss Joel. That came out of nowhere. I need to know what he's doing or if he's dead in the doorway of a bar somewhere or if he's thinking about me the way I'm thinking about him. And now all of a sudden, I can't think about anything else.

—Mia

March 17, 2089
Day 199, year 11

The shuttles are up and running again, which means I was able to get to the hospital today. I haven't been in four weeks, and everyone was very concerned when they saw me, but I assured them I've felt fine and nobody needs to worry about me.

My memory is getting worse. I failed the memory test today for the first time. The nurse who administered the test looked sad for me but said that, unfortunately, memory loss was going to be inevitable in my case. It was a wake-up call for me. I knew I had been forgetting things—leaving my door unlocked, accidentally getting off at the wrong shuttle stop, forgetting my best friend's name—but when a bunch of doctors in lab coats tell you that you're losing your mind, it all starts to feel pretty official.

Joel hasn't answered any of my calls. I've limited myself to calling him only three times, and I refuse to go looking for him in his apartment. I will not be desperate. He either wants to be with me or he doesn't. I can't change his mind either way.

I don't know how much time I have left in my body or in my mind, so I decided today that I'm not going to waste any more time. I went over to Jonah's place to borrow his computer. I needed to find someone, anyone.

It only took a few minutes to make an online profile for myself. I decided against posting my picture and my age. I wanted to be as discreet as possible.

For hours, I looked through image after image of various men. Jonah looked over my shoulder and scowled at the holograms that popped up. I wonder if he realizes how ugly he is. He has to, right? I guess if I were as ugly as him, I'd be jealous of everyone else too.

You can't be picky, I told myself. You just need a person that lives somewhere other than here. So I started sending messages. I must have messaged a hundred of them, pretty much anyone who lived at least an hour's transit from me.

Then I waited.

And waited.

And waited.

And then suddenly, a message popped up.

Danny Correll wants to chat with you!

I stood up so fast that I knocked my chair over, and Jonah yelled at me to be careful. Frantically, I ran to the bathroom and assessed my appearance. My hair was frizzy, my face was makeup-less. This would be a disaster.

I sat back down in front of the computer and hastily tried to come up with a disguise. I pulled the hood from my jacket up over my head. It covered my forehead where most of my age lines are, and it hid the gray in my hair. I scrolled through the various filters on the website and found one to put over my hologram. I stared at the image in front of me, tilting my head different ways, trying to find the angle that would make me look best. I took a deep breath and felt sudden freedom. I could be anybody I wanted. I could be a sad widow looking for love or a lonely artist who never found her muse or a divorced mom of three looking for revenge on her ex-husband who took the kids and ran.

I didn't have to be Mia Einecle.

I clicked "accept." Less than ten seconds later, my image shrank and flew down to the corner of the screen, and then there he was.

Danny Correll. My first experiment.

He was bald, chubby, had round glasses, a brown mustache, and wore a uniform that made it clear that he worked in some sort of office. He was completely unremarkable. He would be perfect.

He seemed nervous. His voice was high-pitched, almost feminine. We were only able to chat for a few minutes before Jonah shouted that he needed his computer back.

"Well," Danny said, "shall I come visit you? Or…is it too soon? Should we message again a few more times?"

"No, no," I reassured him. "I'd like to see you. But I'd rather travel to you, if that's all right."

He seemed surprised, but he smiled. "Well, sure. Okay."

"Tomorrow?"

He swallowed, and his eyes looked like they were going to pop out of his face. "Um, okay. Yes. Here, I'll send you the address of a good bar here. Could we meet at seven?"

I opened the link to the bar. It takes ninety minutes by shuttle. Perfect. I wrote the address down in my notebook. "I'll see you tomorrow, Danny. At seven."

"Yes, yes. Looking forward. Okay. Bye, Mia."

And that was it. I have a date tomorrow night with a stranger. It will probably be terrible. I will probably be reckless and stupid and drunk. I might even have unprotected sex. Who knows? *Carpe diem*, right?

—Mia

March 31, 2089
Day 213, year 11

Has it really been two weeks since I wrote anything in here?

It's been an interesting two weeks, I can say that for sure.

Danny turned out to be completely uninteresting, which I had expected. But I got to get out of my neighborhood and see new things. He was too shy to invite me to his place, and I wouldn't have gone if he'd asked. I never answered any of his messages. I don't have the time to waste on him. I feel this sense of urgency for once. I don't have to stay in my apartment all the time. I don't know how much time I have left, but at least I can fill it to the brim with as much life as possible.

I cut my hair up to my shoulders and dyed it black to cover up the silver. I slather makeup on my face when I go out. I bought tinted glasses to hide my eyes. I look like a completely different person, dark and mysterious and maybe even a little sexy.

I've been checking my messages at Jonah's every day and agreeing to meet every man I chatted with. I have dates every night, sometimes more than one and always with a different person. Some of them stand out. Most of them don't.

Collin was forty-five, handsome, and recently divorced. He spent the entire evening talking about his ex-wife then asked if I wanted to have sex in the bathroom. I left without saying goodbye.

Andreas suffered from PTSD and was only dating because his therapist had told him that he needed to put himself out into the world and be vulnerable with another person. I told him his therapist was wrong and he should find a different one. He cried, and I felt bad and offered to pay for our drinks.

The most tempting offer was from a guy who never told me his real name but went by Bud. He showed up to our date with his wife. They were looking for a three-way partner, he had said. Was I interested?

I kissed Juniper once. I had asked her if I could, and she asked why, and I told her I just wanted to know what it felt like to kiss a girl. So she let me. Her lips felt small and timid, and it was nothing like kissing Elliot.

I studied Bud's wife. She had frizzy hair like mine, but hers was red. Her arms were tattooed with all sorts of birds. She wore a top that showed off her breasts unapologetically, and I have to admit they were pretty impressive. Her eyes were coated in black liner, and her lips were painted dark purple. I imagined what they would feel like against mine; would they be like Juniper's? Would they taste like purple lipstick? Would I feel exhilaration? Would I feel guilt? Would I feel nothing?

In the end, I decided against it. I'm sixteen, after all. I can barely have sex properly with one person, much less two. But they were kind to me and paid for my dinner and told me to call them if I changed my mind. Who knows? Maybe I will someday.

Throughout all this, there's been one guy, only one, that has really and truly intrigued me enough for me to ask him for a second date. His name is Sam Stone. It sounds like a made-up name, which makes him even more intriguing to me. Unlike the others, Sam insisted on visiting me at my apartment. He lived far away, he said. He didn't want me to have to take a two-hour shuttle ride. He would be happy to drive. When he got to my apartment, the first thing I noticed was how much younger he looked in person. He had told me he was thirty-five, but he didn't look a day over twenty. His hair was long and blond and held back neatly in a ponytail. He was attractive in a generic, toothpaste commercial kind of way, and yet I couldn't help feeling like I had seen his face somewhere before.

He arrived in time for dinner, and he complimented me on my lasagna. We talked the entire evening, and before I knew it, it was three in the morning. I asked if he wanted to stay the night, and we were both surprised by my boldness. He said he was fine to drive home but said he really, really wanted to see me again. He flashed his toothpaste-commercial smile at me, and it was enough to make me melt. I told him I would think about it.

And I did think about it, today on the shuttle. I'm supposed to have a date tonight with a new guy that I can't even remember the name of, but maybe there's no point in doing that.

When I got onto Jonah's computer, I had a long message from Sam. He went on and on about how much he enjoyed our night together, about how he thought I was stunning and elegant and he couldn't stop thinking about me, and he knew it was short notice but would I be able to visit him tonight? He attached the shuttle information and told me he would meet me there if I said yes.

I know it's stupid, but I'm flattered. I'm flattered that Sam Stone, an attractive and successful bachelor, wants to date me. And I've been a hypocrite so far, saying that I want to live life to the fullest and then only going on dates with people that I know for a fact won't go anywhere. That's the opposite of full. It's completely empty, and it's starting to get boring.

I messaged Sam and told him yes. I will meet him tonight.

I've decided to take my notebook with me on a date for the first time, but I've promised myself that I won't write in it until afterward. Who knows? He might ask me to stay the night. I can't just *not* write about something like that, you know?

I want to say "wish me luck," but I don't know who I'm talking to. This notebook? People in the future who may or may not ever read this? My own self?

Oh, well. It doesn't matter. Just wish me luck.

—Mia

April 5, 2089
Day 218, year 11

Deep down, I've always thought that humans are the worst and are only out to hurt each other. I've never believed anyone who said they loved me. It wasn't *me* they were after, just what they could get from me. My friends talked me down from the ledge of paranoia so many times. I would run and hide from them, sometimes for days, but they would always find me and reassure me that they really, truly loved me. We were family. I ran from them a lot in the beginning of our friendship. They always ran after me. "As long as we are alive," Jorge would tell me, "you will always be loved." So when they died, any chance of me finding true love died with them.

I know who Sam Stone is now. And I know what he really wanted from me.

I'm writing all this from a hospital bed in a city that I don't remember the name of. I've slipped in and out of consciousness for five days. I'm just now feeling well enough to write down what happened.

I met up with Sam in this city like we had agreed to do. I hadn't ever visited it before, and I was nervous. But Sam greeted me at the shuttle stop with a smile and took me by the hand.

"Come on," he said. "There's a beautiful spot about five miles from here where you can look out and see the entire city. It's breathtaking, especially at night. I'll drive us."

It had been a while since I had been inside an actual car instead of the shuttle. Sam's looked brand-new. It seemed to breathe itself to life with the press of a button. "Good evening, Sam. Where would you like to go?" the car asked, and Sam gave an address, and then we were zooming in and out of traffic, and I just stared out the window admiring all the city lights while he told me about his day.

Eventually, the car pulled into an abandoned parking lot and turned off. "Are you sure this is the right spot?" I asked skeptically.

Sam nodded. "Yeah. We just have to walk up that little path over there. It's about a five-minute walk, and then we'll be on top of the hill."

After that, my memory is hazy. I remember him squeezing my hand as we climbed, and I couldn't tell if I was imagining it or not, but his grip seemed to tighten the farther that we walked. At that point, I knew something bad was going to happen. I also knew that there was no way I could run. My only chance was to fight. I looked around wildly as he pulled me up the hill; there were stones, tree branches, a couple of broken glass bottles here and there. My adrenaline started kicking in, and I felt like I was going to black out, but I forced myself to keep going.

We made it to the top. I don't remember what the city looked like. I don't remember if we were sitting or standing. But I'll always remember the look on his face when he said, "I had a little brother. Did I mention him before?"

No. No, he hadn't mentioned his little brother before.

"Yeah. He died earlier this year. People always told us we looked alike." His face swirled in front of me. I had seen this face before on someone else. "His name was Cap."

Cap.

Short for Copernicus.

Copernicus Ethan Stone. Age seventeen. Murdered on day seventy, year 11.

I frantically reached for anything I could find to fight with, but I was no match for Sam, and with every blow to the head, I retreated deeper and deeper into my subconscious. I would be dead right now if it weren't for another couple who happened to climb the hill a few minutes later. Sam ran off and left me. The couple called emergency services. I woke up in this hospital bed.

I had missing teeth. My eyes were swollen shut. Sam had broken five of my ribs, fractured my skull, and ripped out part of my hair. I'm recovering pretty well. I always was a fast healer. The doctors brought in a dentist to fix my teeth, and today, they told me I can finally eat something.

The police officers asked me if I knew who had done this to me and if I would like to press charges. I lied and told them I hadn't seen his face.

I'm not mad at you, Sam. You did what you had to do. I didn't know Cap. I had never seen him before that night. Maybe he was a good person. Maybe he read poetry when he thought nobody was looking. In any case, you loved him. His parents loved him. That's more than I can say for myself.

I need to rest now. I need to get better, and I need to get out of here.

—Mia

April 8, 2089
Day 221, year 11

Untitled
A poem by Mia Einecle

I saw a beautiful face at my window, but she had no eyes.
So she couldn't see how desperate I was to make her love me,
or how the smell of her hair made my skin tremble,
or how one single touch of her fingers
could turn hot to cold or cold to hot.
She couldn't see the sunlight pouring out from every inch of her,
covering my bed in streams of white and gold.
She couldn't see me.
She couldn't see anything.

I saw a beautiful face at my window, but she had no mouth.
So she couldn't tell me that she didn't feel anything when I told her I
loved her.
She couldn't tell me how lonely she was.
She couldn't tell me how the sky looked darker every day
and nothing made sense anymore
and how there were so many ugly things following her
whenever she turned around.
She couldn't tell me anything, and I never asked.

I saw a beautiful face at my window, but she had no ears.
So she couldn't hear me scream and beg her not to go.
She couldn't hear music or the sound of the blood rushing through my
head
as I watched her sway gently back and forth, back and forth, back and
forth from my rafters.
She couldn't hear anyone crying for her.
She couldn't hear that she mattered.
And even if she could, she wouldn't have listened.

I saw a beautiful face at my window.
But it was only for a moment, and then she was gone.
Sometimes,
I wonder if I imagined her.
Sometimes,
I wonder if she imagined me.

—Mia

April 14, 2089
Day 227, year 11

Okay, remember a few days ago when I said I didn't want to know anybody ever again?

I still mean that, I think. Maybe. I don't know.

So many things happened today I can't keep my thoughts and feelings straight. I just got out of the hospital two days ago, and today, I had to go right back for my regular checkup. My head has been aching all day. I told my doctor about it. He said it was most likely from the head injury I had suffered, but he would run a few scans just to be sure. My brain looks fine for now, but before I left, he told me to pay attention to the headaches and keep track of frequency and severity.

My other injuries are healing well. Miraculously well, even. The swelling in my face has gone down. I can breathe without feeling agony. I wear a scarf around my head to hide my patchy hair. For the most part, I look the same as I always do, just slightly more battered than usual. I don't mind. I actually kind of like it. It reminds me of when the five of us would get in fights and nurse each other's wounds and go to school the next day proudly wearing our battle scars and silently screaming "don't mess with us."

After the appointment was over, I made my way to the front desk to check out. The same front desk girl has been there every time. I never bothered to learn her name, but I do know that she is twenty-five, is allergic to peanuts, and has a boyfriend named Jasper. Normally, she gives me a pleasant smile, reminds me of my next appointment, and that's that. She's not exactly friendly, but she's always been professional. Until today. Today, there was no smile. She wordlessly handed me the screen that I needed to sign and yanked it back when I was done. She couldn't look me in the eye. I waited for a moment to see if she would give me her usual "see you in two weeks," but she just sat there silently. Slowly, I began to back away from the desk, but right as I turned to leave, I heard her say, "You deserved it."

I turned back. She was glaring at me. Her eyes were red and watery.

"You deserved it," she said again, this time with more conviction. "Sam should have killed you."

There was no one else in the waiting area, no one to save me from her.

"Did you even know Cap? Did you even know the kind of person he was?"

Breathing came in short bursts like a fish out of water, my lungs hammering against my broken ribs.

"My little sister was his girlfriend. They grew up together. They loved each other. He wanted to marry her after high school. People say high school sweethearts don't really exist anymore, but that's not true. They were the real thing. He was a beautiful person. He made her so happy. He didn't have an ounce of violence in him." She was out of her chair now, pacing behind her tiny desk. "You destroyed so many lives. So many lives. And soon, you're going to die. And I hope it hurts, and I hope you die alone."

Every two weeks.

I've seen her every two weeks: her smile, her white button-down shirts, her sparkling eyes whenever she took a call from Jasper.

This whole time, behind those eyes, she's been wanting me to die alone.

I turned around and shuffled away. I made it out the door and onto the sidewalk before I sank to my knees and cried. I cried for Cap and everyone who still loved him: his brother, his girlfriend, his parents, his friends. My ribs ached and my head started to throb as I slowly got back up onto my feet and turned to walk toward the shuttle stop.

I deserved them. Every sting of every cruel word. Of course, I deserved them.

I missed the shuttle that I normally took. Another one would come in twenty minutes. I sat down to wait and rest my aching legs.

And then I cried. Not uncontrollably, not loudly, but enough to let my emotions slowly trickle out of my body and into the air. I just wanted one person. And no matter how hard I tried not to want another person, I knew I couldn't do this alone.

Do you believe in God? I never gave it much thought. I didn't think God would be all that concerned with me, if he or she existed at all. But maybe I've been wrong.

Because then, I heard a voice.

Not God's voice. That would be crazy.

It was a voice I recognized.

"Mia?"

He stood there, not ten feet away, looking like his heart was breaking at the sight of me. He was thinner, his face sunken in, his skin gray and ashy. But his eyes were the same. And his voice was the same. And when I stood up in shock, his smile was the same.

"God, I'm so happy I found you," he said with a sigh of relief.

He had gotten my calls. He had wanted to call me back. He had gotten sick and needed to spend time in hospital. Then the blizzard happened. He had tried calling me back, but my phone was turned off. Then he tried calling Jonah, but no one answered. Then he went out looking for me, but he couldn't find me. And nothing he said mattered to me then because he was there now, at the exact moment I needed him most.

"Joel." I breathed out his name. And then I was in his arms, and I began kissing his face, his hands, his lips. He was surprised, but he didn't resist, and then he started to kiss me back. And we stood at the shuttle stop kissing and crying and laughing.

I have a feeling that most people don't get what they deserve. I know I didn't, not today. And I'm so, so happy for that.

—Mia

April 16, 2089
Day 229, year 11

Joel came back with me to my apartment after we met at the shuttle stop, and he has yet to leave. He sleeps next to me in my bed at night. It's a tight fit, but we don't mind. We've spent the last two days just basking in each other's presence, soaking up the energy that we create simply by being near each other. We drift in and out of sleep. Time has stopped feeling relevant. We sit in silence, and then we talk for five hours straight. And it is all so effortless. He's like an extension of my own self. I barely notice he's here, and I can't imagine him gone.

Today, he asked me if I remember the first night we spent together. I told him yes, of course, I did. He had leaned his head back and closed his eyes and asked me the question that I know had been eating away at him for weeks: "Why did you leave?"

Jorge.

I wake up every morning and silently repeat his name to myself like a mantra. *Jorge. Jorge. Jorge.* I'll probably forget my own name before I forget his again. But I will always remember how it felt that night. The night I forgot it.

"It wasn't you," I blurted out. "It had nothing to do with you."

"Okay." He looked me in the eyes. "What was it about then?" He didn't press. He waited patiently until I sorted out my thoughts well enough to express them out loud.

"I had a friend named Jorge," I finally said, and then it all came spilling out.

Jorge's family.

Jorge and T.

The party.

The boys in the alley.

The night my world ended.

Joel sat and listened, never interrupting, never taking his eyes off mine. When I finished, he only had one question: "Do you remember his last name?"

I nodded. "It was Martinez."

Joel's face changed. His eyes clouded, and his mouth clamped into a tight line. "Did his mom ever work as a housekeeper?"

I nodded again. "Yes."

He turned white and looked like he was about to be sick. "Shit," he whispered. "I knew him." And then a single tear rolled down his face. I've never been able to do that, to manage to have just one tear come out of my eye. It's such a beautiful way to cry, the socially acceptable way, the way that won't make anyone stare uncomfortably. It's not my style. I either have waterfalls pouring from my eyes and snot from my nose or I have nothing at all. But Joel is able to pull of the single-tear-down-the-face cry. It's both devastating and sexy.

I grabbed his hand. "Are you sure?" I asked.

"Yeah. I know exactly who you're talking about." He sighed and rested his head on my shoulder. "When they talked about those kids on the news, the ones that got killed that night, I had no idea he was one of them."

"How? How did you know him?"

It's true what I said before about Jorge: to be known by Jorge was to be loved by him. Whether you saw him every day of your life or you met him once in passing, his energy stayed with you like a scar. Joel remembers him. He told me the story.

"His mom worked for us. She cleaned our house for years. We knew she had a lot of kids, but we never met any of them. Until... there was one day. She called and said her oldest kid had been suspended from school and she had to bring him with her to the house. So she came over with her kid. He was small. Younger than I was, maybe twelve or thirteen. I was sixteen, maybe seventeen. I must have stayed home sick or something that day because I was at the house. Or maybe I had gotten suspended too. I honestly don't remember. I was a little shithead punk in school, and I got suspended all the time. But this kid, he didn't look the type. He was quiet, and he did what he was told, and he seemed scared of me for some reason. So I decided to talk to him. He was a good kid. He told me he had gotten suspended for fighting. He had been sticking up for a friend. I told him he had done the right thing. He left with his mom, and I remember thinking he was special. Something about him was better than anyone else I knew. I would see him in the halls at school every now and then, and I would always smile and wave, and he would wave back... I don't know. I guess I didn't really 'know' him. But I feel like I did."

We looked at each other and didn't say anything for a bit. He got up eventually and began pacing the floor; I got up and locked myself in the bathroom. I curled up on the floor and sobbed. I let every memory I had of Jorge pass through my mind, my heart, my body. Each time, it felt like a knife stabbing, stabbing, stabbing—a million invisible stab wounds across my chest.

"Mia?"

I heard a soft knocking on the door. "Mia? Are you okay?"

I took a deep breath and stood. I told myself to put the knives away, to only take them out when I was numb and desperate to feel something. Otherwise, it was all too painful. I opened the door, and Joel stood there facing me.

"You did," I said.

"Did what?" he asked.

"You did really know him," I answered, and slowly, I wrapped my arms around his neck. "Everyone who talked to Jorge knew him. He held nothing back from anyone. That's why we all loved him."

Joel buried his face in my shoulder. "I'm glad," he said. "I'm glad I knew him."

"I'm glad you knew him too."

We stood there in each other's arms, right in my bathroom doorway. It felt ridiculous. Neither of us wanted to be the one to pull away from the other. And when we eventually separated, I felt his energy still clinging to me, just like Jorge's had always done.

—Mia

April 22, 2089
Day 235, year 11

Stammer
A face, a feeling,
Blood rush, cold feet, a kiss, a stammer—
And then, all at once, things change.

Loose lips make new neighbors
and melt whitewashed windows.

In time,
there will be no stone unturned.

The secrets are not secrets.
The curtains are not curtains.
And all of a sudden, this home you built,
in years, in tears,
it sways on its foundation and eventually falls.

Now,
These stones become warnings that your lips can't take back
And you've grown old, so old
Because of that face that's no longer a face, but a reminder
that even strong things can break.

I met Joel at his place tonight before we left for drinks, and I was snooping through his things while he was in the bathroom (I know, I know, how terrible of me), and I found a folded-up piece of paper at the bottom of one of his drawers. I don't know why, but I shoved it into my pocket before he came back out and took it home with me, and I just now opened it.

It could have just as easily been written by Matty. The form and the lyricism are so similar. But at the very bottom of the page was a simple inscription: Joel, August 31, 2087.

My face is no longer a face. It's just a reminder that even strong things can break.

It's something that you can understand only if you've been aged, if you've had years of your life taken from you, if you wake up from a three-week-long nap in a body that you don't recognize.

I've been getting a lot more headaches lately ever since that night on the hill. Sometimes, they go away quickly. Most of the time, they last for hours. They make me dizzy, and all I can do is just lie down on my back with my eyes closed until they pass. I feel like my brain is slowly rotting, turning black, molding, oozing, smelling like death.

I'm doing everything in my power to make sure I always remember my friends. For the last four or five mornings, I wake up and whisper all their names out loud over and over—Jorge, Matty, Juniper, Elliot, Jorge, Matty, Juniper, Elliot—and then they eventually all meld together like one word: Jorgemattyjuniperelliot. I repeat it like a magic spell, those four names, the only things I care about remembering. Yesterday, I accidentally whispered "Willow" instead of "Juniper," and it took a few moments before I realized my mistake.

Willow looked nothing like Juniper. She was a tiny little wisp of a person with short, thin hair and a timid smile. But their eyes were the same. All five sisters had the same eyes: bright blue irises with hazel rings around the pupils. I want to remember those eyes. I want to remember all of my friends' eyes. Jorge's were deep and dark, Matty's were light brown, and Elliot...those green eyes, his hair, his smile. I still remember him, every inch of him. I can see him on the back of my eyelids. I can hear his laughter when I think of our drives to the ocean. I can smell him: Irish Spring soap and a hint of weed.

Smell keeps more memories than any other sense. I was on the shuttle once, waiting for it to move, and a kid who looked about fifteen or sixteen walked past where I was sitting to take a seat behind me. And I smelled that smell, unmistakable, unforgettable. It was so strong that I knew Elliot had to be there, no matter how impossible that was, and I waited, waited, *waited* the entire shuttle ride for the inevitable moment when he would plop down into the seat next to mine and play with my fingers. He had the softest hands. The shuttle lurched to a halt. The kid behind me stood and left, but his smell stayed with me for the rest of the day.

—Mia

April 28, 2089
Day 241, year 11

The dizziness has gotten worse. I can barely sit up without vomiting. Jonah gave me the week off work and was kind enough to escort me to the hospital today. The doctors took more scans of my head, but they didn't need to. I could have told them what was wrong. Deep down, I knew I had a brain tumor.

Actually, I have several.

The scans showed five or six tiny ones. They hadn't been there two weeks ago.

I'm a little surprised that I don't care more. My doctors care. They all looked somber as they surrounded me and discussed treatment options. Radiation is the best option. It will destroy my body, but it will hopefully destroy the cancer too.

Hopefully.

I was given medication to manage the pain and dizziness. It will make me sleepy, but at least I'll be able to move around a little bit each day. From now on, I'm going to have weekly visits to the hospital instead of biweekly ones. I'll have my first radiation treatment at my next visit.

I remember when Joel told me that he had cancer. He was so nonchalant, so straightforward. And after he told me, we just sat and drank and talked about nothing. I want to tell him about me, but I don't know how. I can't just come out and say it the way he did. Maybe I'm still in denial. But I'm not going to tell him just yet or even worry about what I'm going to say when I do. For now, I think I just need to rest.

—Mia

May 1, 2089
Day 244, year 11

Today, Joel asked if he could show me something if I promised to keep it a secret. We went back to his apartment because he said he couldn't show me in public and risk it getting seen by someone else. He had told me to keep my eyes closed. There was some shuffling around, a drawer opening, the "thud" of what sounded like a wooden box being dropped onto the floor, the sound of papers being rummaged through.

"Okay," he finally said as I heard him make his way toward me. "Open up."

The very first time I saw Elliot, I was thirteen years old, and it was my first day of eighth grade. He walked into my English class, the last class of the day, and sat in front of me. It was the only time in my life that the mere image of someone had made everything else around me freeze in place. I don't know if I believe in love at first sight, and I especially don't believe a thirteen-year-old can experience it. I didn't know Elliot. I didn't know his hopes and dreams and fears or anything about him that mattered. I wouldn't call it love at first sight. I would call it…*awe*. I had never seen such a beautiful human before, and I couldn't imagine seeing anything or anyone else for the rest of my life that stirred up the same emotion that my first sight of Elliot did. Then I opened my eyes and saw what Joel was holding up in front of me.

It was a picture.

Of him.

Not like his picture on his ID card. This was a drawing, an actual pencil-on-paper drawing, of him at nineteen, or maybe even eighteen or seventeen, whatever age he was before he got aged the first time. The drawing was beautiful. *He* was beautiful, and he looked alive and real, as real as the boy living inside his thirty-five-year-old body. His hair fell in thick waves across his forehead, his cheekbones were sharp and defined, his mouth formed the same smirk he always wore, except now it finally suited his face. I looked at the drawing, then up at his face, then back to the drawing.

"It's beautiful," I said finally. Never had there been a greater understatement. He smiled at me, and I saw it: the resemblance between the two faces. I saw the boyishness in his face, a boyishness that had always been there but was hard to see unless you were really searching for it.

"Are you wondering how I got it?" he asked.

I don't know if the law banning the personal possession of any images of your face is still in effect by the time you're reading this. The government promised it would be temporary, but the government is also full of bullshit. Right now, the only images of our faces that we are allowed to keep are the ones on our ID cards. The pictures are retaken every year on day one, and the old pictures are disposed of, never to see the light of day again. Our younger faces exist only in our memories. It was a law that was passed when we entered the New Age. Before that, people actually used to own their own cameras that could capture their faces. People would take pictures of themselves at birthdays and graduations and weddings and sitting in bars drinking with friends, and then suddenly, cameras were banned. Every home was inspected, every personal device was wiped clean. Our pictures were destroyed. There was no evidence that any of us had ever existed as anything other than what we were *right this second*. We are whatever our picture says we are. No smiles. No editing.

There is only one picture from my childhood that I still remember. It was a picture of me, my mom, and my dad at the beach. We had taken a vacation the summer that I turned four. It was my first time at the ocean and the only time I think the three of us were truly happy as a family. My parents had printed out a big copy of the picture and hung it on our kitchen wall. I would look at it every day and remember the taste of the salt in the air and the feeling of sand between my toes and the sound of the waves rushing toward my ankles and then pulling themselves back. Then we had to take the picture down and destroy it. I didn't see it happen. I just came down for breakfast one morning, and the picture was gone and the wall was big and empty and sad. It was the first time I had ever felt my heart break.

I turned to Joel. He smiled and traced the edges of the paper gently with his finger. "I drew it," he said simply, taking the paper and carefully placing it back in his desk drawer. "I'm an artist. Or I *was* an artist. I was planning on going to art school and everything. This was the last drawing I ever did. I needed a self-portrait for my portfolio, and I didn't like any of the ones I had made before. Self-portraits are *really* hard to do, Mia. Did you know that?"

I shook my head no.

"Well, they are," he continued. "Our own faces are harder to draw than pretty much anything else because they are the only things that are impossible for us to see, I mean to *really* see. Not like in a mirror or a photograph. We can't see our own faces, not like other people can. So we have to just…draw, whatever we feel is our truest self to us."

He took my hand and led me away from his desk and onto his bed. "I was always good at drawing faces. That's what got me in trouble the first time. I was arrested for making fake ID cards for people. So no art school for Joel. They took all my drawings. Years and years of my life and work, they just took it. But I couldn't let them take my face." His characteristic smirk played across his lips. "So do you know what I did? I took my face, and I ripped open the lining of my jacket, and I sewed my face inside of it, and when I asked for my jacket back after I was aged, they just *gave* it to me! No arguments. Can you believe that? Anyways, I know it's nothing compared to what they put you through, but they aged me five years the first time. All of a sudden, I didn't recognize my face anymore. I had a few gray hairs. I had bags under my eyes. And this apartment was all set up for me. I've been through two more agings since, and I've always come back here, and it's kind of comforting, knowing that at least this place will stay the same every time I come back to it. But that first time, coming here, when everything was new, I felt so lost, Mia. I don't think I left my bed for three days. I smashed all my mirrors. I couldn't stand to look at myself. And I kept trying to open my jacket up, but every time I tried, I just couldn't bring myself to do it. I thought about just burning it. What was the point of keeping my face anyway? What the hell had I been thinking? If someone caught me with it, I'd be in trouble. I could be aged again and again and again…"

Joel was rambling. He did that sometimes, and I was happy to let him. But his voice trailed off, and he seemed lost, like he didn't know where to go next. So I jumped in.

"You did open up the jacket eventually though," I replied. "Why?"

He shrugged. "I got drunk. Really drunk. And I just ripped it open, without even thinking about it. And I saw my face, and I started *sobbing*, Mia. I mean I absolutely lost it. Because my face was so beautiful, and I got to keep it and look at it whenever I wanted. I've looked at it so much that it's burned into my brain. It doesn't matter what anyone else sees when they look at me. I know the truth." He pulled me toward him so that we were lying side by side, his arms around my shoulders and my legs intertwined with his. "Everything about my life has fallen apart these last few years. But damn it, Mia, I'm so happy I have that picture."

We squeezed each other's bodies as tightly as possible until we made a human clump of arms and legs and torsos, but it still wasn't enough. I wanted to be *inside* him somehow, to crawl inside of his skin, his body, his soul, to live in his mind and stay there forever.

"I want you to draw me," I whispered suddenly.

Joel shifted his position to look at me. "You want me to draw you," he repeated.

I nodded emphatically.

He smiled but shook his head. "You are beautiful, Mia," he said. "Nothing they will ever do to you will change that." He reached up and stroked my jawline with his fingers. "But this face isn't yours. This is the face they gave you. If I'm going to draw you, I need to draw the *real* you." He tilted my face to the right and to the left, carefully studying me, and I couldn't bear to look him in the eye.

"My real face is gone," I whispered. Joel pulled my face toward his and kissed me, and all I could feel was his teeth against my lips because of how big his smile was. "That's not true," he said. "Trial information is all public record. Video recordings are all saved in government buildings. We can go to the courthouse downtown right now and ask to watch your trial, and they'll just hand it over. It's your right as the condemned, you know. Remember all the stuff they said to you when you were first convicted?"

They had read me my rights. I hadn't listened to a single word.

"Come with me. Please." He grabbed my hands. They were sweating. "Let's go right now. I want to see your face."

And that's how we ended up at the courthouse downtown watching my trial unfold, and even though I had been the center of the whole thing, it still felt completely unfamiliar to me. Most of the time, only the back of my head was visible, bent down in shame. But then there was one shot, only about two or three seconds, of my face. And Joel immediately stopped the recording.

It was my face. *My* face.

We both stared at it, unflinching. There was no emotion in that face, just hollow, expressionless eyes and pale dead skin. But Joel was transfixed. He sat there for ten minutes in total silence just taking it all in. "Okay," he finally said.

"Okay, what?"

"Okay, I think I've got it," he said.

He was still lost in his own head as he grabbed me by the hand and pulled me toward the exit. He didn't say a word while we walked back to his apartment. He didn't say a word while we climbed the stairs. He didn't say a word when he pulled me onto his bed and kissed me, long and deep, before taking off his shoes and pulling out a pencil and paper.

"You aren't doing this *now*, are you?" I asked in disbelief.

He shrugged. "I don't have to if you don't want me to," he answered. He smiled and traced my jawline with his thumb. "Don't worry. I won't forget your face. I couldn't forget it even if I wanted to."

I kissed him again. "You're a smooth talker, you know that?" I said.

He raised his eyebrows. "Maybe I should be a bit more careful then," he replied.

"I don't want you to be careful." I rolled his body onto mine. "I'm not fragile."

He looked down at me, eyes shining. "No. You're not," he said. And then it happened.

We were naked. The lights were on, illuminating every wrinkle, every blemish, every scar. I didn't care. I wanted him to see everything.

Nobody ever talks about your second person. Everyone always talks about the first one, what you should do and say and expect. But nobody tells you what your second person will feel like. So I'll tell you what it was like for me.

You love him completely but not exactly the same. The motions are familiar, but he holds you slightly differently, and his torso isn't quite as narrow and he whispers things into your ear when you would rather him stay quiet. And the whole time, the *whole* time, you can't help but compare him to your first.

When it was over, Joel put his arms around me and asked me how I felt, and I told him the truth—I had been thinking about Elliot the whole time. I told him how sorry I was and that I understood if he was upset with me. Joel wasn't upset though. He wasn't offended. He actually smiled and kissed the top of my head.

"Thank you for telling me," he said as he sat up and awkwardly began pulling his clothes back on. "I'm not Elliot. I never will be. And I don't ever want you to think you have to choose between us. You can have us both. You already do."

So there it is. I have Joel. I have Elliot. But I can't figure out if there's enough room for both of them.

—Mia

May 5, 2089
Day 248, year 11

"Just relax," the nurse whispered to me as she jabbed the needles into my arms, turned, and left.

Today was my first day of my new cancer treatment. I was placed in a chair surrounded by thick glass. A large machine sat right outside the glass with tubes that entered my little chamber through a vacuum-sealed opening in the glass and connected with the tubes in my arms. I felt sort of claustrophobic, but they gave me something to calm me down, so I slept through most of it. It's amazing all the stuff they can pump you full of if you just ask for it. I told the nurse I felt sick to my stomach.

"Oh, I can give you something for the nausea," she offered from outside the chamber, and then she grabbed a vile of something and put it into my IV.

Then I told her my skin felt itchy. She had something for that too. I asked for stronger pain meds; I got them. It's been a few hours, and I'm still feeling high. I haven't felt this good in a long time.

The treatment area is tiny—five of those chairs in the glass boxes on one side of the room and cabinets full of drugs on the other side—and it really only has room for patients and doctors, not visitors. That did nothing to dissuade Joel. He stood on the other side of my glass box for the first few hours, constantly getting scowled at and told he was in the way by the nurses until I finally was able to convince him to leave. Sometimes, I like him more when he's not actually with me. He's just so…*clingy*. And he worries about every little thing. And he makes me feel like I'm incapable of doing anything on my own.

"Are you sure you'll be all right?" he asked during one of my bouts of consciousness.

I nodded. "I'll be fine. Go home and relax."

He stood in place, looking around anxiously, unsure of what to do. I didn't say anything else, just closed my eyes and drifted back off to sleep. When I woke up again, a nurse was unhooking me from the machine, and Joel was nowhere to be found.

I'm home now. I feel weak, but otherwise, I'm fine. My body doesn't hurt. I feel calm and relaxed. The fog in my head has cleared, and I'm finally able to write.

Radiation treatment, the doctors have been explaining to me, has improved greatly over the last eleven years. I'm not a scientist, so I don't really care about the reasons why. I know that older radiation treatment was hell. It attacked every part of you. You couldn't eat. Your hair fell out. Even your connective tissues would start dissolving. It involved pain, lots of pain. It isn't like that anymore. My hair won't fall out, they said, and I might only have some mild aches and pains. However, since my body has already been through so much as a result of my aging procedure, there is a good chance that this treatment could do damage to my already unstable blood, bone, and muscle cells. But they all assured me that it would be worth the risk. So I'm trusting them.

What else can I do?

—Mia

May 6, 2089
Day 249, year 11

I've slept for twenty of the past twenty-four hours and still feel like I could sleep twenty more.

Joel was at my apartment before I was, ready and willing to get me everything I needed. It was a nice gesture, but the only thing I really wanted was to just be alone and rest. So I told him that he didn't need to stay, that I was just going to be sleeping the whole time and I didn't have the energy for any conversation. He said that was okay, and he would stay with me anyway just in case I needed anything. I was too tired to argue and just let him stay.

Jonah and I have become sort of friends, I guess, but he's also my boss and landlord. I know I have to work if I want to keep staying here. The new treatment is making that impossible, and I used one of my few waking hours to tell him that.

"You know that the stipulation for you being here is that you clean and maintain the other apartments," he had replied. "Those aren't my rules. They're the government's."

I felt a knot form in my throat and panic rising up to meet it. But then Jonah's eyes softened just a little bit. He yanked off a fingernail with his teeth and spat it into his carpet. "This is going to stay between you and me. Got it?" he finally said. I nodded. He continued. "For now, you do whatever you can handle. If you can work six days a week, great. If you can manage three, that's okay. If you can't manage any…well, that's the way it is. Whatever you can't do, I'll do for you. You'll still get your stipend. You'll still have your apartment. I'll tell that arrogant cheap-suited bastard who comes by every month to ask me about your performance that you're doing just fine and I'm perfectly satisfied with your work. Understood?"

The relief I felt was so overwhelming that I could barely manage to whisper a "thank you." Jonah went back to scowling his normal scowl and turned to check on a mess of sausages and onions sizzling in a pan on his stove.

"Why are you doing this?" I eventually asked.

He kept at it in front of the stove, not looking at me, just salting, peppering, stirring. "You could use a break," he said simply. "And I don't dislike having you around."

Coming from Jonah, that was practically a declaration of love. I couldn't help myself. I walked up behind him and wrapped my arms around his massive waist, not bothering to try to get my hands to touch. Jonah spun around angrily. "What are you doing?" he shouted. "You're going to make me burn myself!"

But when I turned to leave, I glanced back at him, and I saw his scowl soften just a little bit.

—Mia

May 8, 2089
Day 251, year 11

For the first time in three days, I actually feel kind of good. I'm not stupid. I know it's not because of the treatment. It's too soon for that. But as long as I'm feeling good, I don't care if it's just from the placebo effect. I have energy. I'm happy. And Joel wants to take me out tonight, so I am trying to find something to wear. I have this one outfit that's good for a night out: a black dress, bejeweled sandals, and a sweater if it's cold. The rest of my wardrobe consists of oversized flannels and T-shirts and baggy pants. I hate the feeling of anything digging into my skin. My clothes looked fine on a teenage body. Now that I'm a middle-aged lady, they make me look like someone's crazy grandmother.

I'm sitting on my bed staring at all of my clothes piled up on the floor, wondering if I could get away with something more daring. I used to be daring. I snuck into Elliot's room one night wearing nothing but a raincoat that was quickly removed. Could I get away with something like that now? I do have one pair of jeans that are tight and that I never wear. If I wear a loose-fitting top with them, maybe they could work. And if I do really heavy makeup and if I put my hair up so the gray doesn't show so much… I don't know. Maybe, I could manage to look sexy. I'm in a sexy mood. I've been thinking about Joel all day like a giddy schoolgirl with a crush. I feel happy for myself. I don't know… I guess I'm doing well, and I'm proud of myself for doing well. I want to go out and look good and get drunk and have sex. I deserve it. I deserve to be happy.

—Mia

May 13, 2089
Day 256, year 11

The second round of radiation wasn't much different from the first: not a lot of pain but a lot of exhaustion afterward. Joel stayed with me the whole time and made sure I got back to my apartment safely. He made me food that I couldn't manage to eat and fetched some extra socks for me when my feet got cold.

During one of the few hours that I was awake today, I sat outside and soaked up the sunshine. It's been getting warmer outside, getting ever closer to the always magical day 275. The first official day of summer. The start of the last season of the year. It used to matter to me, but I don't think it will really feel like anything special this year. All my days feel pretty much the same lately.

If things had gone differently, I'd be getting ready for senior year to start, and Jorge, Juniper, Matty, and Elliot would be with me. We would have gone through the last year of school together, counted down the days until graduation together, and then counted down the days until we all turned eighteen, or nineteen in Jorge's case. And then we would have all run away together and explored the world together and grown old together. Elliot and I would have gotten married. Juniper and Matty would have fallen in love with each other eventually; I was always sure of that. Jorge would have found the boy of his dreams. I was always sure of that too. We would all have gotten to be in love and free and wild and happy. All of us, together.

No, Mia. You're just being wistful now. Because the truth is, I don't think Jorge could have ever left his mother behind. He would have lived with her until she died. And Juniper wouldn't have abandoned her sisters, and Matty wouldn't have abandoned Juniper. But Elliot... Elliot would have gone with me.

No. Don't think about Elliot. Every time you do, it feels like your heart is getting ripped apart in the blender that Dad used to use to make his smoothies every morning.

There's someone I haven't thought of in a while.

Dad.

He's getting ready to become a father again. He would have gotten the nursery ready months ago at Mom's request. They both did everything absurdly early. I wonder if Mom is driving him crazy. I wonder if he's working out as much as he did when I lived there. I wonder if he misses me. I wonder if he even thinks of me at all.

My head is spinning. I can barely keep my eyes open. I don't want to go through all this again next week. I don't want to spend whatever time I have left with my eyes shut and my teeth clenched. I don't want to sleep my life away. I just want to be free. That's really the only thing I've ever wanted.

—Mia

May 18, 2089
Day 262, year 11

I never did fully recover from last week's radiation. I sleep more than I'm awake. And I still feel exhausted. And tomorrow, I have to start it all over again. "It will be worth it, Mia," Joel says. "The treatment will work. You'll see. Just a few more weeks, you'll see." He says "you'll see" a lot. I don't know what it is I'm supposed to be seeing. He's all but moved out of his own apartment and into mine. He sleeps next to me in my tiny bed. He goes shopping for us. He only talks to me when I talk first, but he's always here.

I think I really do love him.

From the moment I met Elliot, I knew there would never be room for anyone else. I knew he could never be replaced. I knew I could never let him go. But that's the beautiful thing about Joel. He doesn't demand anything. He doesn't need much space at all. He simply fits into all the tiny cracks of my heart that Elliot doesn't occupy, like water fits into a jar of marbles. He smiled at me when I told him how confused I was about it all.

"That's how love works, Mia," he said simply. "Love doesn't take up space. It doesn't crowd. It doesn't push anything out. It does the opposite, it makes your heart bigger and bigger until you can fit the whole world inside of it." Then he kissed me on the forehead, and I fell asleep in his arms.

—Mia

June 2, 2089
Day 276, year 11

Two weeks. It's been two weeks since I last had enough energy to pick up a pen and write.

I skipped radiation today. When I woke up this morning, I felt a pounding in my head that was a combination of one of the frequent headaches I've been getting lately and a voice repeating over and over, "Don't go, don't go, don't go."

The pain is getting worse. They said that would happen; I would feel worse before I feel better. They assured me it was normal. Last week's session left me with a sharp pain in the back of my skull and feeling weaker than I've ever felt before.

I couldn't bring myself to tell Joel. He's been so happy that I'm getting treatment. He's convinced that I'm going to be cured, and he's dedicated most of his time lately to taking care of me. This past week, I could barely walk around without getting so dizzy that I puked everywhere. He never said a word about it, just quietly cleaned up after me. "It'll all be worth it," he would whisper to me as we wrapped ourselves around each other each night.

I knew I would have to come up with a plan to get out of the apartment without Joel following me, and it hit me as I sat up in bed to watch him fix breakfast. "Joel," I said sweetly, "do you know what I would love more than anything today?"

He was aggressively scraping something in a pan with a spatula. "What would you love, my dear?"

"Remember that special soup you made me that one time? The one with the homemade chicken stock and the tomatoes and all that?"

I could tell he was frowning even with only the back of his head in view. "That's kind of an all-day project. And I don't have the supplies. And we need to leave for your appointment soon…"

"Well, can't you get all the stuff from the market while I'm at the hospital? And you can work on it while I'm there, and then it will be done by the time I get home?"

"I wouldn't be able to go with you to the hospital at all then."

Exactly, I thought. "That's fine. I'm fine to go alone. I'm so tired I'll probably sleep through the whole treatment today anyway. You don't have to be there to watch me sleep."

He sighed and approached me with a smile. "If that's what you want, then I'd be happy to make it for you," he said, planting a kiss on my forehead. So apparently, it's not all that hard to fool him, although I did feel bad that he would be spending the entire day cooking for me after I lied to his face.

I caught the shuttle to downtown, but instead of getting off in front of the hospital, I stayed in my seat. Buildings, cars, trees, clouds, they all blended together like watercolors bleeding into one another on a canvas. I closed my eyes and leaned forward. I would take the shuttle to the ends of the earth, and I would sleep through it all. On the shuttle, I was anonymous. I was just some lady in baggy pants and an oversized sweater with the hood pulled up over my head. No one noticed me. No one spoke to me. No one even sat near me. It was a peace that I hadn't felt in a while; the peace that comes with solitude.

I woke up right as the shuttle pulled into the stop by my apartment. I hadn't moved in hours. My neck was protesting against any movement. I dragged myself onto the pavement anyway, shuffled the few blocks to my building, and opened my door only to be hit in the face with the overpowering smell of basil. Joel's face was red.

"I think I overdid it with the seasoning," he explained.

I smiled and put my arms around his waist. "We'll make it work," I replied, and together, we slowly added some water to the mix.

It bubbled and steamed and my glasses quickly turned into useless panes of fog. I was able to eat some of it without throwing up after. After we finished eating, Joel fell asleep on the bed with the lights still on. I sat down on the couch, felt a sudden burst of energy, and pulled out this journal to write and write and write before the energy goes away. It feels so good to be writing again. Maybe, I'll go back to treatment next week. I probably will. But today, it was nice to just escape, to exist, to clear my head. Today, it was nice to just be.

—Mia

June 7, 2089
Day 281, year 11

I'm forgetting. I'm forgetting everything. My memories are bubbles, and every time I desperately try to grab one, it bursts in my face. I try to stay perfectly still and let the bubbles swirl around me. They still pop anyway, one by one, and soon, I won't have any left. It's the medicine that's doing this to me. It's killing the tumors, and it's killing everything about who I used to be in the process. My brain is a vapor. My friends' faces have no features. My mother is nothing but a shape, a black cloud that burns me when I touch it. The three boys, the gunshots, the blood on the ground, it's all a dull grayish color.

I've spent all day rereading everything I've written in this notebook. I don't remember writing any of it. I've kept the notebook tight against my chest until just now so I can write in it, afraid that if I loosen my grip, everything about me will disappear except for what I am right now in this moment. But that's what the government wants anyway, doesn't it? That's why we can't have photos. That's why we all turn a year older on the same day. That's why we are the age they say we are and not the age we truly are. My past selves don't matter. None of our past selves matter. We are who we are today, and nothing more.

—Mia

June 9, 2089
Day 283, year 11

"We missed you last week, Mia."

Those were the first words out of the doctor's mouth when she saw me today. She seemed annoyed, but she was doing her best to hide it.

"I'm sorry. I just couldn't manage to get myself out of bed," I offered carelessly.

She squinted skeptically at me but quickly moved on. "Well, I have some good news for you," she said with a smile. "We took some brain scans today, and it appears that the tumors are shrinking."

I had no reaction. She continued, "This is exciting, Mia! This is what we had hoped for. We can't remove the tumors surgically. You would be at high risk for severe brain damage, possibly memory loss, and worst of all, death."

No. She had it backward. Memory loss is worse than death.

"So, Mia, you should have a very comfortable next several months, provided that you keep up with your treatment…"

"I don't want any more treatment," I blurted out.

She didn't believe me at first. She just patted me gently on the leg. "I know it's tough," she said, "but you can't give up now. You're doing so well! I know it's hard to remember that…"

"Have you ever had brain cancer?" I interrupted.

She stiffened at the question. "No. I haven't."

"Then you don't know."

Feigned concern and half-hearted pleading followed. I wasn't budging. I'm never going back to that place again. I'll die a slow, painful death, but at least I'll still remember everything.

—Mia

June 10, 2089
Day 284, year 11

There are exactly zero stars in the sky tonight. Normally from my window, I can see at least four or five, but tonight, it looks like someone painted over the sky. It's just black, black, black as far as I can see. Even the moon is quiet; a small sliver of it is poking out shyly from behind a cloud.

My dad is German. I have vague memories of spending time with his parents when I was little. They spoke only German to me, and my little brain had yet to be completely taken over by the English language, so like most children do, I possessed the superpower of magically understanding them. I barely know ten words in German anymore. We spent Christmas Day with them when I was four. We sat on the floor in front of a sparkling tree and sang "Stille Nacht," and I closed my eyes and pictured a sky exactly like this one.

Still.

Silent.

Empty.

I'll never see Joel again.

I told him about my decision to stop my treatment. His eyes turned stormy as I spoke. When I finished, neither of us moved. We sat across from one another like two gargoyles—me crouched on the bed, him balled up on a saggy couch cushion thrown onto the floor. He finally asked me if I was serious. I said yes. He asked me why. I told him I didn't like the way it makes me feel. We went back and forth, back and forth, and each time, he grew more agitated, more urgent, until finally he was yelling. It devastated me. He had never yelled at me before. It was our first real fight, and it would turn out to be our last.

He said I was choosing to die. He said I was selfish. He said I was choosing myself over him. He asked if I had even thought about him at all, about how he would feel. And I told him the truth: no, I hadn't. It never once occurred to me that making a decision about my own body would need approval from someone else. I have no desire to answer to anyone. I don't want to be needed. I told him those exact words. He just buried his head in his hands and sobbed, and between sobs, he told me that he couldn't see me ever again. He couldn't watch me give up and die. He loved me too much. He needed to forget me and move on. Calmly, I stood, a thousand things that I wanted to say racing through my mind. He was a coward. He was a hypocrite. He was the selfish one, not me. But when I opened my mouth, only two words came out: "Get out."

He grabbed his things without saying a word. He didn't turn to look at me when he left. It felt like it was happening to someone else. It didn't even feel like it was happening to a real person. It was like watching a scene from a bad movie.

He's gone now. He's all gone. And he left me with nothing except the last words he ever said to me, "Forget and move on."

—Mia

June 13, 2089
Day 287, year 11

It's been three days, but I'm still here. I'd be lying if I said that my heart wasn't in pieces. Living has consisted of only two things: sleeping and not sleeping. When I sleep, I usually dream of Joel, but not always. Sometimes, I dream of Elliot. Sometimes, I dream of Mom. Once I dreamed of Detective Gavin. We were back in the interview room, both of us completely naked, neither of us caring. The subconscious mind is like a sea full of garbage. A single wave can bring you dead animals, glass bottles, used condoms, nothing that would ever go together otherwise but somehow makes sense when you see it all together for a few moments.

When I'm not sleeping, I stare at the ceiling in agony. I alternate between crying and gathering up the strength to cry. I cling to denial: I never loved Joel, not really. I lie to myself: I'm better off without him. I stripped the sheets off my bed and piled them on the floor so that my mattress is as empty as I feel. I write things down and then tear them out and throw them away. Maybe, I'll tear this page out too.

I've given myself three days to mourn. Tomorrow, I'm getting up and leaving. I don't know where I'll go, not yet. I'm going to get on the shuttle and never get off. I'll sleep on it, like the other homeless people do. Jonah can give my apartment away. He can find someone else to do his cleaning. I don't need to work; I can beg and steal money for food. I don't know anything beyond that. But if I really do only have a few months left, I sure as hell won't be spending them here.

—Mia

June 14, 2089
Day 288, year 11

Six in the morning.

The sun is beginning to rise. The last few of the previous night's club-goers are slowly being replaced by this morning's working class, the ones whose taxes pay for the free transportation for people like me. But it's the least they can do after the price I've paid to society, isn't it? I've taken a seat by the window in the back and silently claimed it forever as my new home.

This is my favorite kind of space, the kind where you can be surrounded by people while being entirely alone. The shuttle lurches forward, heads tilt down, eyes dart everywhere to avoid making contact with others. I might as well be invisible.

The shuttle will stop in Newport first. It's home to a crappy shopping mall, drug dealers, and ten to fifteen different strip clubs. I've passed through it a thousand times on the way to other places, but I've never stopped there. It isn't the kind of town anybody goes to on purpose; you just sort of end up there after a lot of alcohol and poor decision-making.

I like to play this game with myself whenever I ride the shuttle, where I study the people around me and come up with a backstory for them. To my right, we have Melinda. She's a twenty-five-year-old nurse with a secret drug habit. She has a live-in boyfriend named Todd. He wants to marry her, but Melinda isn't so sure. She hasn't told him about the drugs. He almost caught her once—she had just finished snorting a line of coke when he walked in the apartment unexpectedly—but she was quick enough to hide the evidence. She feels like a hypocrite every day. She wants to quit. She wants to tell someone, but she knows that if she does, she'll lose her job, and Todd might leave her. I'm sorry, Melinda. I'm sorry that you feel trapped. I feel trapped too.

In front of Melinda is a forty-something, well-groomed lawyer in a blue pinstriped suit. He would have a name like Jonathan Steele or Judd Walker or Jonas Bonds, something with a J, something no-nonsense and manly but only at the office. To his friends, he's simply Jay. He has it all—money, fancy cars, good looks—but he's still looking for love. He's stingy with money, the kind of guy who yells at people for leaving the bathroom light on and who takes the shuttle to the office so he doesn't have to pay for parking. He's cool and confident in the courtroom, but he always panics on first dates. He was in love once, a long time ago, but he gave her up in order to fully pursue his career. She's married now, and it kills him, and he's afraid that he will never be able to love anyone the way he loved her. I'm sorry, Jay. I know how it feels to lose your one true love, but I don't know what I'd do if I had to watch him marry someone else— Elliot, all grown up, married, with three kids and a big house and a dog named Ferris—I would break. I'm not as strong as you are, Jay. I couldn't get on this shuttle every day and go to work and go on dates and drive my fancy sports cars and pretend to be happy and success-ful knowing that Elliot was in love with someone else.

The shuttle doors open, welcoming a new passenger. It's Devon, a biology student and closeted lesbian. She makes it a point to only listen to music that no one has ever heard of and gives up on bands once they become too mainstream. She's proud of the fact that pop culture doesn't influence her music choices, completely missing the irony that pop culture does influence her music choices, just in the opposite way. She refuses to shave her legs as a statement against the patriarchy. She's in love with her brother's girlfriend and writes sad songs about her. She tries so hard to be genuine that absolutely nothing about her is genuine. She is nothing but a conglomerate of anti-conformist ideals. I used to be like that too, Devon. I acted like the world couldn't touch me even though in reality it touched me too much. I hope you learn to be yourself someday, Devon, not just an idea of yourself.

I always wanted to be a writer, a real writer. I wanted to write books. I thought I would be good at it. But now I'm looking back at these people, my characters, and they all suck. They're bland, one-di-mensional, shallow. A nurse secretly addicted to drugs? A lawyer searching for true love? A girl who has yet to discover who she really is so she just makes something up? They've all been done before, a hundred times.

I want to ask Melinda what her real name is, but, no, I'm too late. She just got off at this stop. In Newport. All this time, her destination had been Newport. Maybe, I was right about the drug habit after all.

I don't have anything else to say for now. I'm just going to close my eyes and take this shuttle as far as I can.

—Mia

June 14, 2089, evening
Day 288, year 11

I slept for a while, but I'm awake now. I haven't moved from my seat for the past fifteen hours—haven't eaten, haven't slept, haven't peed. I've been too distracted by the scenes outside my window. It's been a long time since I've seen so much of the world all at once. This shuttle goes in a giant circle, and I've gone around the circle four, no, five times now. Each time, I see something different. No one else stays on the shuttle longer than thirty minutes before getting off. Hundreds of people have seen me and ignored me. I'm thankful for that today.

Juniper and I used to ride the shuttle together whenever we wanted to go see a horror movie at the theater. The guys were all terrified of horror movies, but Juniper and I loved them. We met our fair share of creeps on the shuttle. We were propositioned for sex. We were called names. We were told that we needed to repent of our sins and believe in Jesus Christ. Pretty much any and all kinds of encounters. Sometimes, we enjoyed the attention. Sometimes, we ignored it. Every now and then, we would get angry. We always came away with good stories to tell the guys.

What I really need right now is money. I'm faced with an uncomfortable choice: do I beg or do I steal? Who are my targets?

Melindas. Jays. Devons. The Melindas would shun me. The Jays would be too oblivious to notice if I helped myself to the contents of their wallets. The Devons would give me money and make sure that everyone else saw them do it.

My hands are shaking. I'm not ready. Not yet. My own money will have to do for now. I'll get some food, and then I'll get some more sleep, and when I wake up, it will be tomorrow.

—Mia

June 15, 2089
Day 289, year 11

The rain started last night. Raindrops on my window lulled me off to sleep, and raindrops on my window woke me up this morning. I shut myself in the tiny shuttle bathroom for a few minutes to brush my teeth and put on a different shirt. I don't own many clothes, and I brought most of them with me. They're all the same; I know I've said it before, but I really only like big, shapeless, bland clothing. Big flannel shirts. Loose linen pants. Giant sweaters. In summer or winter, in rain or shine, I always drape my body in clothing that covers every inch of me. I don't have a bad relationship with my body. It's the opposite, actually. I feel a weird ownership over it. It is mine to show and mine to hide. Only the people I deem worthy may see it and judge it. Everyone else gets to see a dark shapeless mass.

Elliot was the first person who ever saw through the shapelessness and saw me. He always told me that true beauty could never be hidden. Writing it down makes it sound so lame. It wasn't lame when he said it. I wish I could explain how it sounded. I wish I could describe his voice in general. It was high-pitched and manly at the same time. It was never loud but always confident. It was gentle. It was musical. It was as smooth as marble and as warm as a stone sitting in the sun. It was the voice that Jesus Christ used to introduce himself to Mary Magdalene. I hope that gives you an idea.

We would get looks when we were out together, lots of looks. We didn't make sense to anyone else but us. We didn't belong together. I noticed how girls with his same brown skin would look at him: with desire. And I noticed how their eyes would slowly go from him to me, and their eyes would always say the same thing, "How dare you take him from us?"

Maybe, that sounds strange to you. Maybe, you are reading this a long time from now and the color of your skin is no more important than the color of your eyes and hair. But right now, it matters. It matters a lot. People like to pretend it doesn't, but it does. The darker your skin is, the more likely you are to be targeted by law enforcement, to get convicted, to get aged. To be killed. To be called a "nigger" by some asshole. To have a white girlfriend become so enraged by it that she just starts shooting, shooting, shooting...

No. Don't think about that night. Not here. Don't think about how if you hadn't fired that gun, Elliot would still be alive. Don't think it. Don't say it.

The shuttle slows to a stop. People leave. People get on. And I'm still here. I've been here since Elliot died, watching people move forward, getting where they need to go, while I stay stuck in place.

Tears fall down my face, and I match my raindrop-covered window. No more words today.

—Mia

June 16, 2089
Day 290, year 11

A shuttle driver has finally noticed me.

I asked my dad once why the person in the front seat of the shuttle was called the "driver." The shuttle drove hundreds of people around, yet we weren't all called "drivers." But if we all started running down the street, we would all be called "runners." And if we swam in the ocean, we were all "swimmers." It didn't make any sense at the time. That's when he told me his drunk driving story and explained to me what driving used to be like. He told me about the old cars from back then and how people used to actually have to press pedals and turn wheels to control them. You couldn't just tell your car *where* to go, you actually had to make it go there yourself. Only one person at a time controlled the pedals and the wheel, and that person was called the driver. And old shuttles were the same way.

Someone had to control when the shuttle would stop, how fast it would go, and where it would end up because the shuttle didn't have the technology to know how to do all those things on its own. And then I remember feeling terrified, and I asked, "But what if a bad person controlled the shuttle? What if he drove it into a building on purpose just to kill everyone inside?"

Dad assured me that those things never happened, and when he was growing up, the shuttle drivers were good at their jobs and always got you where you needed to go. That night, I had a nightmare that I was tied to a seat in a car, and the car had a driver that would make the car crash into a wall on purpose, over and over again.

Of course, there aren't any real "drivers" anymore. The shuttle driver inputs the destinations and makes sure all the software is running correctly. Not the most exciting job in the world, but someone has to do it. This driver doesn't like me. I can tell. I've been on his shuttle for over ten hours without getting off. Legally, he can't make me leave. I've done nothing but get off and on different shuttles for two days, and there's no law that limits how long people can ride them, which is why homeless people practically live on shuttles. Unless you're being disruptive or dangerous, you're allowed to stay on the shuttle for as long as you like. That doesn't mean other people won't notice and get annoyed with you though.

I'm going to have to start getting money pretty soon, and that scares me. You're not supposed to beg on the shuttle. Technically, you're not supposed to beg anywhere. It's illegal, just like stealing is. Isn't that sort of idiotic? Begging and stealing are the same in the eyes of the law. But be honest, would you rather someone ask you for a meal or steal your computer?

Anyhow, that's the problem: I'm poor, I need money, I can't work, I can't beg, and I can't steal. I don't know what the solution is. I've never had to think about it before. My family always had more than enough money. My dad always said it was simple: work hard, get money for it. If that were true, then Jorge's mom should be a billionaire.

I bought a protein bar this morning, and I've been taking little bites of it every few hours, desperately trying to make it last as long as possible. You can never just escape, can you? Your own body won't let you. Anytime you think you've transcended, anytime you think you've truly and completely gotten yourself lost in your mind, your body will always interrupt you eventually with "Hey! Don't forget to sleep! Don't forget to feed me! Don't forget to take me to the bathroom!"

I want to be a ghost. I want to be a disembodied spirit that can go anywhere and do anything for as long as I want. I want to need nothing. I want to *have* nothing. I want to be free from everything and breathe stardust and drink moonlight. I want to find Elliot's spirit, and then I want us to haunt Joel. I want him to wake up every night screaming when he sees our faces at the foot of his bed. And it's all completely ridiculous because I'm writing all this and realizing that somehow, I'm dreaming about living forever even though I feel too exhausted to live at all.

—Mia

June 17, 2089
Day 291, year 11

You know what the worst part is about dying right now?

I won't live long enough to see Orbit Week.

It takes Earth 365 days to go completely around the sun… except that it doesn't. The exact time it takes is 365 days and six hours. Earth doesn't care how incredibly inconvenient that is for humans who want to keep track of days and weeks and years. Earth goes as fast or as slow as she damn well pleases, and no one is going to make her go any faster or slower.

In the Old Age, humans just added an extra day every four years. February 29. The fourth year was called a leap year. Problem solved. But that wasn't good enough for the New Age. There would be no more leap years. Instead, we would have an *entire extra week* once every twenty-eight years: Orbit Week.

Seventeen years from now, Earth will have her first Orbit Week. I'm sure it will be a week of parties and parades and vacations and drunken mistakes. But it doesn't really matter because I'll be long gone by then. So will a lot of people on this shuttle. An ancient woman got on a few stops ago looking like she's being held together with dental floss. She could drop dead on this very shuttle and no one would be shocked. In front of her is a pale, thin man who keeps coughing this ugly, wet cough into his arm. Lung cancer. I know the sound well. There's nothing we can do, the doctors told him. Suddenly, I feel a strange solidarity with Old Woman and Cancer Man. None of us will get to experience Orbit Week. I want to put an arm around each of them and take the three of us far, far away. We'll have our own week. We'll call it the "Week for the End of Time." Anyone who's dying can come celebrate it with us. Rich, poor, young, old, beautiful, ugly, doesn't matter. The finish line of life looms right in front of us all. Death is the great equalizer.

What do you think will happen when the earth runs out of places to bury people? It has to happen sometime, right? The shuttle passes by at least one graveyard every three minutes. What happens when there's no more room in any of them?

I'm not going to be buried. I'm going to be cremated. That much I know. Earth will not get to suffocate me for all eternity. Instead, I'll just disappear into the wind. I'll leave no trace that I was ever alive at all, other than this journal. Think about that, reader. You're holding all that's left of me in your hands. Does that make you feel special? It shouldn't because *I'm* not special. Just find a safe place for me to rest, okay? Don't leave me in the back seat of your car to get bleached by the sun and trampled on by muddy shoes. Is it too late for me to ask that? Have you done that already? Am I all dirty and faded and sad-looking? It's fine. Just try to remember not to do it again.

—Mia

June 18, 2089
Day 292, year 11

This isn't working. This isn't me. I can't stay here. I have a bag of dirty clothes and an empty stomach and a notebook filled with my rambling thoughts. I feel weak. My whole body hurts. So I'm giving up. I already called Jonah. When his hologram popped up, I started to cry because it was so good just to see a familiar face.

"Please, let me come home," I croaked out.

He looked uncomfortable. He hates any display of emotion whatsoever. I stood there waiting for him to tell me off.

"Be back tonight. Knock on my door when you get here," he said. That was it. He got off the phone without saying goodbye, and I felt my knees buckle with the weight of relief.

I'm going home.

—Mia

June 18, 2089, evening
Day 292, year 11

And just like that, I'm back where I started.

Jonah wasted no time giving my apartment and my job away. Lina is young, pretty, and desperate for a place to live and work while she finishes school after being kicked out by her dad. I haven't actually met her yet; I'm just going by what Jonah told me about her.

So what does that mean for me? Well, with Jonah's blessing, I'll be living on his couch for now. "Are you sure about this?" I asked him more than once. He just gave me his classic scowl and told me to quit asking. I told him I would help Lina clean the building. He yelled at me to shut up and just rest. And so, here I am, resting on Jonah's couch.

I don't know what I've done to earn any sort of affection from him. I was a bad tenant. I was an even worse employee. I don't think he sees me as a friend. Does Jonah even have friends?

It feels so good to lie down. My ears are soaking up the quiet like a sponge soaks up water. I haven't had peace in five days. Maybe, I haven't had peace in seven months. Or maybe, I haven't had peace for my entire life. In any case, I feel it now. I have a place to sleep. I have food. I'm free from work, and I'm free from the hospital. I can let out a sigh, and it really, truly feels like a sigh of relief.

"Good night, Jonah," I shouted from the couch a minute ago.

"Good night, Mia," he grunted from his bedroom.

Good night, indeed.

—Mia

June 21, 2089
Day 295, year 11

Jonah ran out of food today.

I've been cooking all the meals for us and eating as little as possible because I still feel bad staying here even though Jonah doesn't seem to mind. Yesterday's breakfast used the last of the bacon, and I used the last egg to bread the chicken for dinner. Jonah came out of his room and stared me down, waiting for me to say something. I started crying. I've been emotional ever since I came back here. I cry at the slightest thing. It's stupid, and I hate it. Jonah sighed and pulled a card out of his wallet.

"Go to that bakery down the street and get us some bagels. Sesame seed for me, if they have them. And cream cheese, lots of it. Then you can go to the store later for groceries." And that was it. He just left his card on the table and went to get the coffee started.

A few minutes later, I found myself inside a tiny bakery that I've passed a million times but never actually gone inside. I don't even think it has a name. In the windows, it just says "BAGELS! DONUTS! PASTRIES!" in big white letters. The smell was overpowering—sugar and flour and coffee and something burning. There is a bakery like this just around the corner from my high school where, during sophomore year, my friends and I would take turns buying donuts for us before class or sometimes instead of class. Those donuts, man, they were everything, perfect little melt-in-your-mouth circles of just the right blend of savory and sweet. I gained ten pounds that year. Totally worth it.

I bought two sesame bagels with cream cheese and brought them back to the apartment. He handed me a cup of coffee when I walked in the door and took the paper bag from my hand, pulled out the bagels, and held one out for me to take.

I shook my head. "They're both for you. I didn't want any. I'm not hungry."

He scowled his signature scowl at me and shoved the bagel into my hands. "Just eat it," he grunted.

I stared down at the paper smeared with a mess of cream cheese and sesame seeds then stared back up at him. Suddenly, he tossed both bagels on the table and grabbed me by the shoulders, not roughly but hard enough to get my attention and for my coffee to slosh around and splash on the floor a little bit.

"I'm only going to say this once, so you'd better listen," he said angrily. "You are welcome to stay here. That means sleep here, eat here, take a shit here. Anything and everything. You can get the groceries, do the chores, whatever you want to make yourself feel better about it, but it makes no difference to me. So eat the damn bagel. Eat the eggs. Eat the bacon. Buy up the whole shitting grocery store for all I care."

I was still in shock from him grabbing me out of nowhere. "I just…"

"Just what? You need money. I have money. You need food. I have food. What the hell is so complicated about it?"

My stomach growled right on cue. Jonah still had his hands on my shoulders and gave me a little shake. "Not hungry, huh?" he grunted. He let me go, grabbed his bagel, went to his room, and slammed the door.

I collapsed into one of the kitchen chairs and put my head down on the table because I suddenly felt exhausted. It's exhausting being in need.

—Mia

June 23, 2089
Day 297, year 11

The weather has been nice these past few days, so I've spent more time outside. I'm sitting on the front steps with my journal and a cup of tea. I don't usually drink tea, but Jonah makes a really good kind with apple extract and honey. He hasn't said much to me ever since the whole bagel thing, but he's been doing all the cooking and always gives me way more food than I can eat.

My appetite isn't what it used to be. I used to eat a lot before the aging, and, of course, my mom never missed an opportunity to criticize me for it. When I was fourteen, I started making myself throw up on purpose, but it didn't really do anything other than make my breath smell and my throat hurt, so I stopped.

To this day, my mother is the only person who has ever criticized my body. Every year, she bought me new clothes for school, always at least two sizes too big, and she'd frown when I held them up and say things like "Are you sure they'll fit? I think they might be too tight. Maybe, we should go back and find a larger size." And I'd insist they were fine, but she'd keep making comments for days afterward even when I wore the clothes and they hung off my body like blankets. I've worn baggy clothes ever since I hit puberty. I want to say it was purely my decision to dress that way, but deep down, I know that she's the reason why.

The doctors weighed me every time I went in to see them. So I know exactly how much I weigh, but I'm not going to write it down because it doesn't matter. I might weigh 100 pounds or 200 or 300 or 600. I'm not telling you because I don't want you to picture me as nothing but a body of a certain size. We are all beyond that. Our bodies are the vehicles that carry our souls around, nothing more. The real you can't be weighed, measured, shrunk down. You are infinity trapped in skin, and then one day, you will be released.

—Mia

June 24, 2089
Day 298, year 11

I just reread that last line I wrote yesterday, and I feel proud of myself for how far I've come. No one can really prepare you for the grief you feel when you know your life is going to end sooner than you were expecting. I went through all the different stages of grief, sometimes more than once: denial, anger (a *lot* of anger), bargaining, depression (a *lot* of depression too). I've finally reached acceptance. The acceptance still occasionally mingles with depression and anger but not as often as it used to. I've stopped thinking "why me?" and instead I've been thinking about how to make the next few months count.

The reality though, and this is something else I'm still working on accepting, is that I don't really have months. I've already noticed more consistent headaches and dizziness. Soon, the pain will leave me unable to move or talk or write or think, and I will have to finish my life alone and in agony and trapped on an old musty couch. I worry a lot that my chance to "make the next few months count" has already passed. I have to stop constantly and remind myself to enjoy the small things because small things are all I have left. The taste of Jonah's apple tea. The feeling of the heavy summer air clinging to me like a familiar blanket. The smell of warm rain on the grass. They are life's little pleasures that never get the appreciation they deserve, and yet they are the ones that stay with you even after everything else has abandoned you. Thank you, apple spice, for the way you dance across my tongue and up my nostrils. Thank you, summer, for being Earth's three-month-long hug. Thank you, rain, for reminding me that tears are what make the flowers grow.

—Mia

June 26, 2089
Day 300, year 11

It's day 300.

Is day 300 still a holiday for you? I honestly don't know why it's a holiday now other than the fact that all the other holidays are gone and we needed a new one.

The only Christmas I remember is the last one. I don't remember much of it, only the tree in our living room with the twinkling white lights and shiny silver ball ornaments and the pine needles all over the floor and my mom drinking vodka in silence while I sat by myself opening present after present wrapped in cheap red-and-green striped paper. There would be no more Christmases after that; nine months later, all holidays were canceled. People could choose to celebrate privately if they wanted to, but our family never did.

Fireworks have been going off since yesterday morning. Almost everyone is drunk and loud and happy. It's hot outside, and the smell of alcohol and explosives is everywhere. My head hurts, but that's not just because of all the noise. Like I said before, I get headaches a lot now.

Jonah is nowhere to be found, but he left a note on the table for me wishing me a Happy Day 300 and a tiny box with a necklace inside. It looks cheap and tacky and exactly the sort of thing a guy who knows nothing about women would buy for a woman. But it was sweet of him to even think of me today. I'm not sure he really has anyone else to think about.

Last year, we all went to Juniper's house for Day 300. Her parents didn't allow fireworks. They were too dangerous. So we piled into the car and drove to the ocean and saw hundreds of fireworks go off across the horizon. We all sat back on our elbows and let the sand envelope our toes and the ocean breeze play with our hair and listened to the *pop, pop, pop* ringing in our ears and throughout the sky. I don't remember the gifts I got them or what they got for me. The gifts never mattered to us. We just wanted to be together.

Today, I'm celebrating by cleaning the apartment. I convinced Jonah to stay out all day so that I could deep clean the entire thing.

I bought some carpet cleaner to try to get the stains out of the floor and some furniture polish for the table. That's my gift to Jonah. He'll secretly be happy, but he won't show it, just mumble an awkward "thank you" and go to his room. He might even smile when he thinks I'm not looking.

—Mia

June 30, 2089
Day 304, year 11

Lina. The new girl. My replacement. I finally saw her today. There was a knock on the door, and Jonah yelled at me from his room to go answer it. I opened the door to find a girl who looked seventeen or eighteen standing in front of me, with soaking wet dark hair and nothing but a shabby towel wrapped around her body. She looked startled to see me. Of course she did. She had been expecting Jonah.

"Can I help you?" I offered casually, doing my best to pretend that a young girl showing up at Jonah's apartment in nothing but a towel was the most normal thing in the world. It took a few seconds for her to answer me. During those few seconds, I carefully studied her up and down.

Ethnicity: vague, maybe part Italian or Greek.

Hair: long and curly even when wet.

Skin: light olive, covered in dark moles.

Large nose, but it suited her face.

Deep brown eyes, almost black.

Full lips, dark pink, almost red.

Shaped like a giant pear, even under the lumpy towel, narrow shoulders, small breasts, and impossibly wide hips.

Thick thighs, but she somehow managed to keep them devoid of cellulite, something I was never able to do even in my sixteen-year-old body.

"So sorry to bother you," she mumbled. Her voice was deep and raspy and reminded me vaguely of Juniper's. "I got locked out of my apartment, and I need Jonah to let me back in."

Intriguing. I racked my brain to come up with a scenario that would possibly explain a young girl, wet and naked, getting locked out of her own apartment: a spider in the shower that sent her screaming out into the hallway, lost keys while skinny dipping, a lovemaking session gone wrong when a pipe burst in the middle of it.

"Is Jonah here?" she asked, but before I could even answer her, I heard Jonah's bedroom door creak open.

"Someone's here for you, Jonah," I said, and then I ran into the bathroom before I saw his reaction. I heard them murmur something to each other back and forth. Then the door closed, and that was it. I crept out of the bathroom. Jonah looked completely normal, like naked women showing up at his door was an everyday occurrence.

"That was Lina," he offered even though I hadn't asked and had already assumed who it was. "She, ah, needed some keys." I nodded. He nodded back.

I've decided that I have to see Lina again. I'm obsessed with her. Not today, not tomorrow, but someday, I'll muster up the courage to knock on her door and ask her where she came from.

—Mia

July 1, 2089
Day 305, year 11

Apparently, Lina wasn't the only person in the building that needed help yesterday because not long after she left, there was another knock on the door. Again, Jonah yelled at me to answer it. Again, I pulled the door open. But this time, I recognized the person on the other side.

Vandré. Apartment G.

He was confused. What was I doing in Jonah's apartment? Hadn't I moved out of the building? Wasn't I fired? "What are you doing here?" was the question he finally asked. For the briefest of seconds, I toyed with the idea of telling him where I had gone and how I came back, but before I could answer, he asked, "Where's Jonah?"

Of course. He didn't want to talk to me. I studied his face; he was in trouble. He had a cut on his cheek, not from shaving; the stubble on his face was at least five days old. His eyes: bloodshot. His hair: greasy. His smell: like he hadn't bathed in a week; stale alcohol and sweat hung like a cloud over him.

"Where's Jonah?" he asked again, annoyed.

I took a step back into the apartment. "Come in. I'll get him."

It was one of the more interesting days I've had recently—a naked woman and a greasy man showed up at the door, both under mysterious circumstances. He shoved past me into the apartment.

"I would like some privacy," he demanded, staring me down.

I stared right back. "You want me to leave?"

"Yes."

"Where do you want me to go?"

He looked incredulous. "I don't give a shit where you go. Just go somewhere else."

"She's staying here."

Both Vandré and I spun around at the sound of the third voice.

"She's staying here," Jonah repeated firmly. I felt like sinking into the floor.

Vandré just got angrier. "What do you mean, she's staying here?" he asked, almost in a yell.

"She is living here with me," Jonah answered calmly. "If you need to talk in private, we can go outside." Vandré opened his mouth to say something in reply, but before he could say anything, Jonah grabbed him by the shoulder and practically pulled him outside, slamming the door behind him.

She is living here with me. Is that what he's been telling people? That we're "living together"? Who would he tell? Why do I even care?

It took a while for Jonah to come back, and when he did come back and I asked him what had happened, all he would say was, "Vandré needed money." And when I asked "what for," he just shook his head and repeated, "Vandré needed money." We haven't spoken since. But the mystery surrounding both Lina and Vandré are far too interesting for me to just forget about them. The second I find out more, I'll write it down.

—Mia

July 7, 2089
Day 311, year 11

Rumors spread quickly in this building. Everybody thinks Jonah and I are dating now. They've all been knocking on Jonah's door for days with various problems: my sink is leaking, my stove isn't hot enough, my bedroom window won't open. Could you please take a look? Please, Jonah? But they didn't care about the sink and the stove and the broken window. They just wanted a peek at me.

Yesterday, Vandré showed up again. He looked better; the cut on his face was healing and his hair was combed and he didn't smell like moldy sweat. "Go get your boyfriend," he said. "I need to talk to him."

I felt my cheeks flush at the word "boyfriend."

Vandré sensed my discomfort and gave me a sleazy grin. "You *are* together, yeah? You are banging him? Having the sex?" Vandré's accent and awkward grasp of the English language made the whole concept sound even worse. "Who gets more drunk before the sex, you or him?" He shuddered and started laughing. "Sorry, I just got a picture of it in my mind. Make sure not to let him crush you to death."

What must Vandré have been like as a kid? He would have gotten away with everything. The good-looking ones always do. He would have tormented me and my friends. He would have been across from us that night. I would have killed him.

I'm no longer who I was that night in November. I'm a shell, a husk. But inside, there are still shreds of that girl with the gun.

My fist flew on its own. I felt his teeth give way, the sting on my knuckles as they connected with Vandré's jaw. He was too surprised to react, just stood there like a broken-faced dumbass while I slammed the door and locked it.

Jonah wasn't even home. He was off fixing someone's broken window or sink or stove. I sat by myself for hours doing nothing. I felt numb and hollow and desperate for that shuttle to come back and be my home again.

I couldn't think of anything to say to Jonah even after he finally came back to the apartment last night. He didn't say anything to me either, just grabbed a beer and took it into his room where he would stay for the night. I laid my head back on the couch pillow and tried to fall asleep. My brain wouldn't let me rest though, not until I talked to Jonah. It was late when I finally summoned the courage to knock on his door. I was scared that he was already asleep and would scream at me when I woke him, but instead, I heard a not-at-all-grumpy voice reply with, "Come in."

Before last night, the closest I had ever gotten to being in Jonah's room was peering through a crack in his doorway. It was the one part of the apartment that I never cleaned. He never told me that I wasn't allowed in or that I couldn't clean it. It was just one of those unspoken rules assumed by both of us. So last night was a big deal in many ways, and going in Jonah's room was the first one.

I sat uncomfortably on the edge of his bed while he sat in his giant chair with a can of beer in his hand, the discarded cans of already-consumed beers crumpled around his feet. He gulped and he stared and he waited.

"There's something I wanted to talk to you about," I finally said. "Not that it's a big deal or anything," I quickly clarified.

"All right." Jonah finished his beer and tossed the can on the ground with the others. "Talk then."

The smell of alcohol mixed with the piles of dirty clothes on his floor is a smell that I won't forget any time soon. It almost made me sick. I don't know how he lives like that, with that smell around him all the time. In Mr. Fuller's class, I learned about olfactory receptors. Smelling something involves literally breathing in particles of that thing. Jonah's beer cans and dirty underwear are inside of me forever now.

"People are talking," I said. "About us."

"What about us?" Jonah asked.

I clenched and unclenched my jaw. "I don't know. They think we're dating or having sex or something."

"Does it bother you?"

Yes, I thought. I stumbled over my answer, "I mean, it isn't true, so…yeah, it bothers me."

Jonah cracked open another beer—*God, how does he afford to drink so much?*—and said, "Well, you shouldn't let it bother you. Just let the little shits talk."

"Did you say anything to anybody? About us?"

I hate that I asked him that. I don't know what even *possessed* me to ask him that. But Jonah didn't seem to care.

"No. Why the hell would I talk to anybody here about anything?"

"I'm sorry. I just…" and my voice trailed off, and somehow, I made it to my next question. "Do you, you know, wish there was anything…about us…to tell?" I wanted to bury myself in the coffee-stained carpet.

Jonah just laughed and shook his head. He didn't say anything.

"I didn't mean it like that," I quickly blurted out.

"How'd you mean it?"

"I meant, you've been a really good friend, and I appreciate that, and that's really all I need in my life right now…" I blabbered on and on until Jonah interrupted me.

"I'm gay."

He said it with complete nonchalance. It took a few seconds for the words to register in my brain. "You're gay?" I repeated.

"That's right." He hoisted himself out of his chair and took a few steps toward me. I've never felt smaller in my life.

"I'm sorry, I didn't know," I murmured.

He just shrugged. "Not many people do," he replied. "Nobody's business. But now you know." He sat down next to me on the bed. I was too embarrassed to look at him. "I don't talk about feelings. It's just not how I am," he said. "That doesn't mean I don't have them. So I'll say this once, and then I won't say it again. Just remember it." He put his hand on my shoulder, and, yes, it felt as awkward as it sounds. But what he said next was really nice.

"I appreciate your friendship too Mia."

And that was kind of it. I left his room and went to sleep on the couch.

It was only the second time that someone had come out to me. I remember the first time: Jorge sat on the floor while the rest of us sat on his couch. He cried. We hugged. I think we all felt closer to each other after that. I don't really feel closer to Jonah. I'm honestly still surprised he even bothered to tell me. I'm glad he did though. I'm glad we're friends. And I really, really don't care what anybody else thinks anymore.

—Mia

July 27, 2089
Day 331, year 11

I haven't written in a while, and that's because there's really not much to write about. I'm still staying at Jonah's, still taking care of the cooking and cleaning, still not entirely sure where I'm going next. The only reason I'm even writing today is to make a note that my headaches are getting worse. And that means that the cancer is getting worse.

I barely had any headaches when I was getting treatment. When I first stopped the treatment, I would get one or two a week. Then they would happen nearly every day. And now it's like I have a constant pain in my head that never goes away.

I'm dizzy all the time. I'm seeing green and purple spots everywhere, like when you stare into the sun and look away. It's hard to even write without throwing up.

Black ink, white pages. Shaky letters. Shaky words. Shaky hands. Everything shakes and shakes and shakes. I'm cold and I'm hot. The smallest sound feels like a car being dropped on my head.

This must be what dying feels like.

—Mia

July 30, 2089
Day 334, year 11

I didn't realize how much worse it could get. My god, it's so much worse.

I can't sit up without the room spinning. My hand is spinning in front of my face…

I just got sick. I keep throwing up. It makes me feel a little better for a few minutes, but then the nausea comes back like a tidal wave over me.

And the pain.

I can normally cope with pain. I can ignore it, push it out of my mind, focus my attention on something else. But not this time. This is a pain I didn't know could exist in my body. This grabs me by the shoulders and shakes me until my neck breaks and I'm paralyzed with nothing but the knives and the fires burning and stab, stab, *stabbing* in my brain. I've never prayed before in my life. But, God, universe, whatever higher power is out there, either take this away or kill me.

Jonah came out and saw me on the couch, and I must have looked pretty bad because I saw sympathy on his face for the first time ever. He rushed back to his room, and I heard him rummaging around in there, looking for something. He came back out holding a small bag in his hand.

"I want you to take this. And I don't want you to ask any questions." And suddenly, there were pills on my open notebook, three of them, small and yellow.

An hour later, they're still there. I haven't touched them. Jonah didn't say what they would do. I don't care if they kill me. I do care if they make the pain worse. Is it possible for the pain to be worse? Yes. Yes, it is. This is what it's like to die of a brain tumor. I asked Jonah only one question, "What are these?"

He frowned at me. He had told me not to ask any questions. "They're called Lionheart," he had said. "They're rare. They're illegal. Don't ask me how I got them. Just take them."

Just take them, Mia.

Take them. Take them. Take them. Make it stop. God, make it stop!
The pills are in my hand. Now they're in my mouth. I'm swallowing them. They're in me now. I don't know what's going to happen, but it's too late to change my mind now.

—Mia

July 31, 2089
Day 335, year 11

I don't feel right. I'm not in pain anymore. But I feel… I don't know how to describe it. It's not like a weed high. Weed always calmed me down, life around me slowed to a crawl, and I felt at peace with the world. This isn't the same thing. I feel confused. I keep having to start and stop writing because I forget the word I'm writing in the middle of writing it. Everything around me feels like it's going too fast. Time keeps on going and going, and before I can grab onto the moment I'm in, it's already gone, and the next moment is here, and then the next moment, and the next moment, and the next… God, I need it to *stop*. *Stop* going forward! Just give me a chance to hang on to something.

Three hours. That's how long it's taken me to write this entry.

I could have done it in only one single moment if moments could just last a little longer. Why the hell is time in such a hurry?

I took more Lionheart because Jonah "accidentally" left it under the couch, and maybe, I didn't take enough before and it isn't working all the way. I don't feel any pain. I don't know what I feel. I don't know if what I feel is even a feeling. How long is a moment? A second? Half a second? Are there moments between moments? And moments between the moments between the moments, and…shit, I just need to lie down. Close my eyes. Close them, close them, close them… eyelids like cement stay stuck in place. Eyelids stuck in place…but not time. Never time. A million moments from the beginning of this sentence to the end of it and they won't stop for anything, and I just want to catch one, just *one*. Is that too much to ask?

—Mia

~~Day 336~~ *Day 337, maybe 338(?)*

This is some good shit. I'm numb all over. I forget how many days it's been. That's okay. I don't need to count the days.

Have I eaten? I don't think I've eaten. Maybe, if I wait long enough, Jonah will feed me. I don't want to move. I can't even remember the last time I got up for the bathroom. I pissed all over the couch and all over myself. And I don't even care! I know I should care, but I don't. I feel like my mind is finally free to not care about anything.

Jonah's not here. I don't know where he is. He left his stash of pills under the couch though. Maybe, he wants me to OD, to be put out of my misery. Is it even possible to OD on Lionheart? It probably is. You can OD on anything if you take enough of it. You can even OD on water if you drink too much… I hate water. Humans can't live for more than three days without water, apparently, but I feel like I've gone longer than that. Or maybe, it's only been a day. Or maybe, not even one day. Maybe, it's still yesterday, and I only think it's today. Man, this is some good shit though. Everything looks red. Red, red, red, like I have red-tinted glasses on or just a lot of blood in my eyes.

What day is it?

Last night, my shadow came to life and tried to strangle me, and when I pushed her off me, she told me I was crazy, but that's a lie because *she* is the crazy one, and she's trying to kill me. And if she kills me, she's going to go around and tell everybody, everybody, everybody that I killed my own self, and no one will ever know the truth. Jonah has come back, or is it a ghost? My shadow told him to kill me. I trust no one, only the stars, because every night, one single star comes down with an elixir to nourish me, and each night is a different star, and each star is more beautiful than the last. They are made up of colors that don't even exist, but I'm never scared, not of them. Will the moon become angry? His star whores keep coming down to me, and he beats them when they go back to him. He is a coward, like my shadow. He only attacks things that are weaker than he is. Stars aren't weak! They only think they are because *he* tells them that, just like my shadow tells me that I'm weak. But I'm not, no,

I'm not... I'm in charge, you have to listen to me. You have to copy me, do what I do, go where I go. You *have* to. You broke the rules. Last night, you broke the rules... I don't want you back. The stars will protect me. Light, light, light, and that's all. No darkness. You can't exist without darkness. You will die, you will be the one that's strangled, you will lay on the ground gasping for breath, and I'll just stand over you and I won't feel sorry, not one bit, because you will never follow me again...

Are we connected? If my shadow dies, do I die with her? If she kills me, will she kill herself? Tonight, I will find out. Tonight, one of us will die. When she comes back to strangle me, I will be ready. I will strangle her first. She will die. Or I will die. Or both of us will die. But then! The stars. They will rescue me...no, not rescue. They will take me with them and make me one of them. I will be a sky light of many colors that no one can describe. And I will kill the moon, and at last, we will all be free...all of us, free...

—Mia

August 22, 2089
Day 356, year 11

I'm here. I'm alive. I'm still me.

Jonah found me early yesterday morning. He said I was passed out and barely breathing, and he couldn't call an ambulance because I still had Lionheart in my system. I woke to him shaking me so violently that I started gagging and throwing up. He said I'd had a seizure and bashed my head on the corner of the table, which explains the gash across my forehead. All in all, I will not be taking Lionheart again. I've learned that there are feelings worse than pain.

Last night, I remember Jonah sitting on the floor next to me holding a cold cloth to my head, and he started rambling. "I know you're still out of it, and you probably won't remember me saying it," he said. "But I'm saying it anyway, and I'm gonna keep on saying it. You need to go back to treatment. You can't handle the pain. I gave you a little bit of something to take the edge off, and you abused it and damn near killed yourself. Do you even know what day it is? No, you don't. You've been completely shit-faced for weeks. You're not yourself. You won't be yourself ever again unless you go back to treatment. Mia, you hear me? Mia?"

Mia.

Mia, what have you done?

I know what day it is. It's day 356. In nine more days, it will be day 1 and everything will start over. I will get a new card, a fresh start.

Jonah says that it will take about ten days for the Lionheart to completely leave my system. I don't know how he knows that. Man of mysteries.

I could go back. In ten days, I could go back. Maybe, I'm not a lost cause. Maybe, the cancer isn't so bad. Maybe, self-sabotage isn't really what I want after all.

Ten days. I have ten days to think about it. Detoxing from this drug is hell, according to Jonah. I won't be able to write. I'll barely be able to think. But when it's over, so will this year be. Year 11. I won't miss it.

—Mia

August 31, 2089
Day 1, year 12

Here we go. Day 1. Happy New Year.

I went to the place you're supposed to go to for your new ID card, got in the line I was supposed to get into, listened to the "snap, snap, snap" of cameras, the whirring of printers spitting out new cards, the grinding of shredders eliminating old cards. My name was called. I slid my old card across the counter. "Snap" went the camera, "whirrrr" went the printer, "grrrrrr" went the shredder, and just like that, I am a new person, reborn, just like everyone else.

I never want to relive what I went through at the end of year 11 ever again. The pain from the brain tumor was nothing compared to the pain of a brain tumor combined with detoxing. I'm still weak today, but I can get up and move around at least. I got on the shuttle by myself, arrived at the government building by myself, even climbed two flights of stairs by myself. Moving my body has never felt so good. I feel sappy saying it, but I'm grateful. It's a new year. I get to start over. I can get healthy. I can meet new people. It's not too late for me.

—Mia

September 1, 2089
Day 2, year 12

I went back to the hospital today. I'm worse, the doctor told me. But I'm still treatable. I'm starting treatment again. Tomorrow, I will go back for the first round, and I'll go back every day for the next five days. We have to be aggressive, the doctor said. We have to give it everything we've got. We can still beat this. He kept saying "we," like he's in just as much trouble as I am.

So it's back to the exhaustion and delirium. Jonah has agreed to come and go with me since I'll be too out of it to even get on the shuttle by myself. Jonah won't say it out loud, but I know he's happy that I'm getting treatment again. He even took me out for a beer since I won't be able to drink for a while after tomorrow.

The last time I went to treatment, Joel went with me. I honestly haven't thought about Joel in a while, but with treatment looming over me, I can't help but remember him. I wonder what he would say if he knew I was going back. It doesn't matter. I'm not doing it for him. I'm doing it for me.

—Mia

September 9, 2089
Day 10, year 12

Well, it's been a while, hasn't it? I guess I should write about what I've been up to.

First, my treatment. It was pretty much exactly what I expected: nausea, fatigue, forgetting my own name. But then I woke up the other day, and everything was just...*gone*. The headaches were gone. The exhaustion was gone. The dizziness was gone.

The pain was gone.

Jonah told me the good feelings were most likely a placebo effect, but I don't care. I feel *good*. That's all I care about.

I found my old dating profile and activated it again. I forgot how much fun dating is. It's so hysterically awkward and exhilarating and, as I found out last night, every now and then, you'll get a good lay out of it. Yes, against my better judgment, I went home with my date. I'm actually still at his place now. It's a lot nicer than Jonah's, although that's true of pretty much anywhere. The sex was good, not great. I didn't feel like doing it, but I sort of felt obligated. It didn't last very long at least. I've never had sex with someone that I didn't love. It's hard to describe what it feels like. In some ways, it's liberating. I didn't really care if he was into it or not. I didn't care what he thought of me. He's nothing to me, just a warm body. He could leave me, and I would feel nothing. On the other hand, it feels pointless. There's no beauty to it, just awkward movements between two people that aren't at all familiar with each other's bodies and don't know how to get around the other person. It's the erotic rendition of accidentally walking into someone on the sidewalk and you both keep stepping to the same side to let the other person pass. It's like hugging someone who really only wants a handshake. It's like telling a joke that nobody gets. I'm not doing this to feel good though. I'm doing it because I can. I know that's a stupid reason. I'm aware, trust me. But it feels good to have the freedom to make bad decisions after I've spent so much time not being able to make any decisions at all.

—Mia

September 13, 2089
Day 14, year 12

This morning, once again, I found myself waking up in a different apartment.

My old apartment.

Lina had taken the time to make it look somewhat nice. There were new pillows on the couch, fresh paint on the walls, bright yellow curtains in the windows. It still felt unmistakably like mine.

It all started yesterday afternoon with a knock at the door. Jonah answered it, and once again, there stood Lina, this time dry and clothed. She said something, Jonah said something, and then suddenly, Jonah was gone, and she was in our apartment, sitting on the couch where I slept every night. I stood frozen in the kitchen while she peered at me.

"I don't think I ever got your name," she said.

Detective Gavin asked me my name once. I told him to think eye, neck, elbow. I was chained to a table.

"I'm Mia," I offered timidly.

Lina smiled at me. "Come over here, Mia," she said. It was like a spell; I had to do what she said. I found myself floating over to sit next to her. "I've heard about you," she said. "You got aged for defending your friends. At least that's what the people in apartment D tell me."

Apartment D. It had been a while since I'd thought of those freaks. "You're one of us, Mia," they had told me after I watched a man's head fly off of his body and roll onto the ground.

"I murdered three boys. That's why I was aged," I replied defiantly.

Lina leaned closer to me. "How old are you? Sixteen? Seventeen?"

I felt my face grow hot. "I'm forty-seven," I answered.

Lina scoffed. She couldn't ask me anything else though because Jonah walked back in with a bottle of bleach.

"Here," he said, handing it to her, seemingly annoyed. "You didn't look very hard if you missed it. Top shelf on the back wall. Literally in front of your eyes."

Lina took the bottle apologetically. "I'm sorry, Jonah. I really didn't see it." She blinked sad puppy-dog eyes at him and looked down at her toes in feigned shame. It had a startling effect on me: heart sped up, hands started to sweat, face began to tingle. Jonah didn't answer, just went to hide in his room like always, and I figured that was it. Lina would leave. Maybe, she would show up again one day needing Jonah's help to put out a fire she started. But she stayed. And my heart kept beating fast and my hands kept sweating and my face kept tingling.

And after a few minutes of silence, she asked, "Do you want to have a drink with me?"

And that's how I found myself sitting across from her in a booth at a bar.

"Here's the thing, Mia," she said after a few drinks. "I didn't need Jonah's help finding the bleach. I just wanted to see you." She smiled. It was intoxicating. My head was buzzing, and it wasn't completely from the alcohol.

"What about the first time? When you showed up in a towel?" I asked.

She laughed. "Oh, that. It's so stupid." She swallowed the last sip of her vodka tonic. "I had just gotten out of the shower. I didn't know what to wear, so I stepped outside, just for a second, to see how hot it was. But then when I came back to the apartment, the door had closed and locked behind me, so…" She shrugged.

I looked at her in disbelief. "Really? That's your story?" I scoffed.

"Yeah. Want me to come up with a better one?"

"Kind of. Yeah."

"All right." She leaned back in her chair and gave me a lazy grin. A slow yawn escaped her lips as she stretched her arms up over her head. The bottom hem of her shirt rode up, exposing a thin white strip of skin. I felt like I was in a trance. "I met a guy," she said. "Don't remember his name, I think it was Ben or Bill or something with a B. He wanted us to go back to his place. I said no, let's go back to mine. I thought, he could be a serial killer, right? No way in hell am I going to his place. So things get freaky. We end up in the shower. I'm down on my knees. And do you want to guess what happened next, Mia?"

I was still too transfixed by her red lips, the sticky smell of sweat and alcohol coming off her, the white skin still peeking through the bottom of her shirt to say anything. "He grabs my hair and starts pulling," she continued. "I'm thinking that he's just playing, but then he starts *dragging* me, like literally *dragging* me out of the shower! He has me by the hair in one hand, and with the other hand, he grabs the wrench I had left on the floor after I fixed a leak under the sink. So I start *screaming*, Mia. I'm screaming at the top of my lungs. And he's telling me to shut up, shut up, shut *up* or he'll kill me. I don't buy it. He looks completely terrified. He doesn't have the guts to kill me. I tell him where my purse is. I tell him to take it and leave. He lets go of me, lets his guard down just for a second. A second is all I need. I grab the wrench out of his hand and start whacking, as hard as I can, over and over and over. Blood starts gushing from his head. He stops moving. I'm still naked and wet from the shower and in shock from what I had just done. When the adrenaline rush started wearing off, I grabbed a towel, and the next thing I knew, I was standing in Jonah's doorway. Imagine my surprise when a strange woman answers his door." She leaned in so close to me that our foreheads almost touched. "How's that for a story?" she whispered.

I didn't back away from her. "Good story," I whispered back.

"Yeah?"

"I mean, it's completely made up, but it's a good story."

She stuck out her bottom lip and pouted at me. "You don't think I could kill someone?"

"No." Two more drinks somehow appeared in front of me. She reached up and slowly traced my jawline with her thumb. "Well, I can. And I have," she replied.

I hadn't had a drink since before my treatment, and the alcohol was hitting me pretty fast. My next memories are broken and blurry, pieces of a puzzle that I can't quite put together. I remember being lifted from my seat. I remember her steadying me as we walked. I remember her tongue occasionally grazing my ear. I remember walking into the apartment that I used to call home and being placed on the bed where I used to sleep. I remember her stroking my hair and eyes. I remember saying "I don't want to." I remember a tingle that spread from my ear across my entire body. She bit my lip; I tasted vodka tonics and blood.

I woke up this morning with a hangover headache, not a brain-cancer headache. I forgot how much nicer hangover headaches are than cancer headaches. I rolled over to see her next to me, naked and asleep, with her impossibly wide hips turned sideways toward the wall. She breathed heavily and soundly as I quietly left without saying a word.

—Mia

September 15, 2089
Day 16, year 12

"I'm so sorry, Mia."

But he didn't sound sorry today when he told me the news.

Yesterday, I went back to the hospital to see how my cancer had responded to the treatment, and, well, it didn't. Not even a little bit. The tumors are still there, bigger than ever. There's no change in my cancer prognosis. According to the doctor, I might be able to make it to day 150 or even 200. After all the grief Joel gave me for quitting treatment the first time, the running away and coming back, the drugs to numb the pain, almost dying, Jonah begging me to try again, that's all I have left. A few months.

I don't know what I expected. A miracle? I don't deserve that.

Jonah didn't come with me today, and I'm glad. My doctor and I are the only people who know. It's a gruesome secret between the two of us. Patient-doctor confidentiality. I wonder how many gruesome secrets he has with other people. Doctors, the ultimate intimate partners. No one else in the world can tell you about the inner workings of your body, can they?

If life had gone differently, I would have been a doctor. I want to look at people and see cells, tissues, organs. I would have trained the humanity out of myself so I no longer saw souls and spirits and essences. People would be as they are on the surface: bones, muscles, blood, sweat, matter that lives and eventually dies. Over and over and over again.

—Mia

September 17, 2089
Day 18, year 12

All of a sudden, I have my own apartment again.

The story of *how* I got my own apartment is so bizarre it's hard to even know where to start. I had gotten home from the hospital to find Jonah completely frazzled, pacing back and forth, shaking. I've never seen him like that before.

"They got him! They got Vandré!" he screamed at me when I walked in.

I just stared at him blankly in confusion. I asked him what he meant: who got him, what happened, where was he now. Jonah crumpled into a pile in the corner and started banging the back of his head against the wall. It felt more surreal than a dream. It took a long time before he calmed down, and I was able to get the story out of him.

It turns out that Vandré was more than just a typical wealthy bachelor who rented a sleazy apartment just so he could have sex with random women in it. See, Vandré was wealthy because he was a scientist. A scientist in a very particular field. And the crazy people in apartment D were on to him. Yep, good old Vandré was one of the hundreds of scientists responsible for the development of the aging procedure, and apparently, he was also the latest victim of apartment D.

Vandré had known he was in danger. The day he showed up at our door with his face all cut up was the day they had tried to kidnap him for the first time. Somehow, he had managed to escape and explained that he was in danger to Jonah.

"Don't use your card," Jonah had told Vandré. "Don't let anyone trace you." He gave Vandré one of his own cards and told Vandré to stay away for a while. They both thought that would be the end of it. Because here's the crazy thing, Vandré knew that there was a group of people targeting the scientists who worked in aging. But he had no idea that those people were his neighbors. Nobody knew a thing about what was happening in apartment D. Nobody except for me. And as Jonah continued to speak, I started to feel sick.

When I got to apartment D, it was empty. Everything had been cleaned out: no food in the kitchen, no mattresses on the floor, no trash left behind. There was no sign that anyone had ever lived there, except for one single VR device laying in the middle of the floor. I'm sure you can guess what had been recorded on it.

It was the same ritual as before: Vandré sat in a chair with a hood over his head, then a man in white slowly walked over, a sword was brought out, it connected with Vandré's head, everything began turning red.

They've vanished without a trace, all of them. They're probably hundreds of miles away by now, set up in some other remote location, continuing their hunt. "You're one of us, Mia. You're *one* of us!"

They had known I wouldn't say anything. But *why* hadn't I said anything?

I think they were right. I *am* one of them. I watched the recording of Vandré's death over and over and felt nothing but relief.

I'm never going to tell Jonah about any of this. But apartment D is vacant now, and Jonah offered it to me. I took it.

I just finished watching the recording on the VR device one last time before deleting it. I wondered if Vandré would be missed as I watched his head roll onto the floor. Blood poured over every surface, and the recording abruptly ended.

Rest easy, Vandré, you piece of shit.

—Mia

September 18, 2089
Day 19, year 12

Whatever you do, never get high and play truth or dare.

Not unless you want things to get *really* weird with your friends.

Our group had a good mix of truthers and darers, which always made the game interesting. Personally, I'm a truther. Ask me anything you want, and I'll either tell you the truth or I'll lie well enough to make you believe that I'm telling the truth. Either way, I don't want you to dare me to do anything. I don't want to be at the mercy of anyone's twisted requests, don't want to be the punch line to anybody's joke, don't want to admit that deep down I'm just afraid of everything and I'd rather talk about myself instead. Matty was a truther like me. We learned a lot about him during those weed-filled truth-or-dare sessions.

"If you had to kill yourself, how would you do it?"

"Jump off a skyscraper. Make a big exit."

"Do you believe in God?"

"I believe there's a higher power. If you want to call it God, that's fine."

"Who's the worst person you've had a sex dream about?"

"Mr. Fuller."

"Noooooooooo!" We all burst into shrieks and fake-gagging noises. Matty just shrugged and smiled, evidently embarrassed by nothing.

Juniper and Elliot were darers. Being stupid teenagers, most of our dares involved them getting naked and doing various things.

"Run to the end of the street and back naked!"

"Jump in the ocean naked!"

"Get naked and don't put your clothes back on till someone says your name!"

Long before Elliot and I started going out, I had seen his penis dozens of times. Maybe, that's why when we finally started having sex, it never felt awkward.

Jorge was a wild card. He made his decisions based on his mood and based on how the game was going for others. "Truth," he said confidently one breezy night as we sat in a circle on the beach. It was my turn to ask.

"What's the hardest thing about being gay?"

Jorge looked at me pensively and didn't answer right away. The other three sat wide-eyed and eager to hear his response. "I don't really know how to answer," he finally said. "It's not something I think about a whole lot. I don't wake up every morning thinking 'I'm gay! I'm gay!' Usually, I think about what I want for breakfast or what I want to wear or how I really need to brush my teeth. Normal human stuff." He paused and started to look kind of sad. "Maybe, that's the hardest part about being gay," he continued. "It's that gay people are really just like everyone else, but nobody cares about that. They'd rather talk about how we're different." He leaned back on his elbows in the sand. "I don't want to be special. I don't want to be a 'hero' just for existing. I don't want to be your gay friend. I want to be your friend. That's it. No qualifiers."

We had all scooted closer to him as he spoke without realizing it. Suddenly, we all clumped together in a group hug. Nothing else was said. Jorge didn't need our words. He just needed us.

Surprisingly, that wasn't the most memorable moment from our truth-or-dare games, or at least it wasn't for me. The most memorable moment happened in Elliot's basement during one of our many basement smoke sessions.

"Truth or dare?" Elliot asked. It was Matty's turn. Elliot had asked the question without much conviction. We all knew that Matty always picked truth. Until that night when he shocked us all.

"Dare."

We collectively gasped and cheered. Elliot looked shocked. He hadn't even bothered to think of a dare for Matty. Matty stared down Elliot with a grin. Jorge threw his arm around Elliot's shoulder. "Do *not* mess this up, man," he said. "We may never get this chance again."

Elliot still looked completely lost. He locked eyes with me. *What should I say?* his eyes asked me desperately. We had only recently started dating and hadn't gotten to the point in our relationship when we could have entire conversations with just our eyes. Five seconds went by, then ten, then twenty. My heart was pounding. What an opportunity! We could finally get Matty to do whatever we wanted! And suddenly, at the same moment, Elliot and I glanced at Juniper then back to each other and smiled.

"Okay," Elliot said. "You have to make out with Ju. For one minute."

Juniper sat across from me casually finishing her blunt. Matty's expression never changed. He just shrugged. "All right," he replied. He looked over at Juniper. Juniper looked back at him. They scooted close to each other. "Who's keeping track?" Matty asked.

"I'll say when," Elliot answered. "Just go. I'll start counting."

And then Matty and Juniper leaned into each other and started planting kisses on each other's lips. I squealed. I couldn't help myself. But after a few seconds, Elliot interrupted. "No, no, no," he demanded. "I said 'make out' with her. Kissing is not making out."

Matty huffed. "Fine. What are your exact specifications, master?"

Elliot took a long drag before he spoke, enjoying the sexual tension he was creating. "Lie down. Use your hands. *Under* clothes." I squealed again, and this time, Jorge joined me.

Matty just rolled his eyes. "You guys are children," he said. But he had no choice. He had picked dare. He had put his destiny in Elliot's hands.

Juniper didn't hesitate. She slid her jacket off, revealing her thin tank top and ridiculously muscular arms underneath. "One minute?" she clarified.

Elliot nodded. "One minute."

Juniper nodded back. She shuffled onto her back and pulled Matty on top of her. And for one minute, they were nothing but a mass of arms and legs and torsos and hands exploring brand-new territory, and yet it seemed so natural that I couldn't believe they had never done this before. I'll let you imagine the rest. I'm not going to lie though. It was one of the sexiest damn things I have ever seen. Either they were in love or they were the best actors to ever exist.

The minute ended, although I'm pretty sure Elliot let them go at it for an extra few seconds. They sat up, wiped their mouths with the backs of their hands, and joined us back in the circle like nothing had happened. Matty and Juniper never so much as held hands after that. Their friendship remained as close as ever, and none of us brought up the events of that night. Sometimes, I wonder if it even happened at all. Weed tends to turn memories into unreliable narrators. But there were all these little things: when Juniper would walk away and Matty would hold his gaze on her just a second longer than the rest of us would or when Matty laughed at something and Juniper's ears would perk up and she would smile ever so slightly when she thought none of us were looking. And I would be brought back to the one minute in time when Matty and Juniper were exactly what they should have always been: one.

—Mia

September 23, 2089
Day 24, year 12

I hate it here. I hate these walls. I hate this big empty room. I hate sleeping on the floor because there's no furniture here at all. My old basement apartment came with furniture. It had a bed. The mattress sagged and the bed frame squeaked, but it was better than the floor. My possessions don't even fill one suitcase. I have my clothes, my bathroom supplies, my phone, my ID card, and this journal. Jonah gave me a pillow and some blankets and a few things for the kitchen. That's it. That's all that's here. That's all I have. I don't leave this room; I haven't left it since I moved in a week ago. I sleep twelve hours a day, I watch movies on my phone, I get food delivered to the apartment and pay for it with money that is quickly running out. Jonah had transferred money to my account a while back, saying that he had forgotten to send me one of my paychecks. It was a lie. I never missed a paycheck. But I took the money and didn't say anything.

I'm realizing for the first time just how alone I am. When I lived in my old apartment, I had Joel. When I left and came back, I had Jonah. Now…now I don't have anyone. No one visits, no one calls, no one sends messages. I could die in this apartment, and no one would notice. I'd be here for years before they found me.

My head is in constant pain. The good thing about being in constant pain is that, eventually, you grow accustomed to it, and it just sort of becomes a part of you. Pain is my oldest and truest friend, with me till the end.

Yesterday, I dumped out all my clothes onto the floor—the dark fabrics, the flannel shirts, the baggy pants, the too-big sweaters that I drape myself with—and I made a nest around myself. They don't smell like me anymore. They smell like the generic laundry soap that Jonah buys for the washing machine. But they make me feel safe.

This might be my last home, the last place on earth that I ever live. I at least want to fill it with as much of myself as possible.

—Mia

September 30, 2089
Day 31, year 12

Most days are unremarkable.

Not only are most days unremarkable, they usually happen all in a row—ten, twenty, fifty, one hundred unremarkable days. Sometimes, you feel like you might go insane if something amazing or horrible doesn't happen, something to just knock you on your ass and break up the monotony of it all.

That's what happened today.

I don't get a lot of messages other than the messages from random guys who find my dating profile, and I get even fewer phone calls. The calls I do get are always spam calls. So imagine my surprise when today I saw a face pop up in front of me that I actually recognized.

It was Joel.

"Hey, Mia," he said weakly.

He looked awful. His eyes and cheeks were sunken in, his skin was pale and lifeless, his collarbones jutted out. He must have lost almost half his body weight. Right away, I knew that he was dying.

"The cancer's gotten a lot worse," he said. "There's nothing they can do for me now."

I just stared at him. I didn't know how to feel. He was the one who left me, not the other way around. He didn't deserve my pity. But looking into those hollow eyes, seeing just a glimpse of the boy I had fallen in love with, I felt myself melt inside.

"They gave me the stuff," he said.

"What stuff?" I asked.

"You know. The stuff. The drugs you can take to, like, speed the process along."

He wants to end his own life. He wants the opportunity to die before the cancer becomes unbearable. And just by looking at him, I know he doesn't have long before that happens.

"Mia, I want you there with me."

He wants me there. He wants me to watch him die.

I couldn't answer. I still can't answer. I told him I would think about it, and that was it. We said our goodbyes, and I cried into my pile of blankets and flannel shirts.

I hate him. I hate him so much. When I was choosing to die, he left me. Now that it's the other way around, he wants me with him.

Why am I even considering this?

—Mia

October 1, 2089
Day 32, year 12

I called him back today. "I'll do it," I blurted out when he answered. "I'll help you die." There was a long pause, then he replied, "Two weeks."

"Two weeks?"

"Yeah. Two weeks. October 15. It's my twentieth birthday. I want to die on my birthday."

He remembers his birthday. I wish I remembered when my birthday was. I wish my parents had cared enough to keep track. It's the least they could have done for their only child.

But that's not true anymore at this point though, is it? I'm not an only child. Mom would have had the baby weeks ago. I wonder if she remembers what day he was born. It wouldn't matter to anybody else. He would have his own little ID card, boasting his little baby picture, his name, and his age: One Year. It doesn't matter if you were born on day 1 or day 365; if you were born in year 11, then your age is one year now.

Joel wants to see me. He wants to spend the rest of his life with me. He loves me. He's never stopped loving me. He told me all this with tears in his eyes, the kind of quiet crying that made him look beautiful and that I could never manage to do myself.

"Do you still love me, Mia?" he asked hopefully.

I lied and said yes.

—Mia

October 7, 2089
Day 38, year 12

I've temporarily moved into Joel's place to help take care of him. He gets weaker every day. He needs my help now with pretty much everything: getting dressed, standing up, eating and drinking, walking to and from the bathroom. Yesterday, he asked me to bathe him. And after all the intimate moments we've shared in the past, it was still so humiliating for both of us as he lay there like an infant, and I tried not to notice when he pissed himself.

This isn't Joel. Joel died the day we swore to never see each other again. This bag of bones is nothing but a husk, the skeletal remains of what used to be a human being, and I'm glad for that. It makes it easier to stay detached from the situation. It helps me not feel guilty for hating him.

Eight more days.

—Mia

October 10, 2089
Day 41, year 12

Joel has stopped eating and rarely opens his eyes. He spends all day flat on his back in his bed like a corpse. He doesn't want any blankets on him. He says they make his skin crawl. He barely needs anything from me anymore, and I've toyed with the idea of just leaving and not coming back.

Today, when I went to check on him, I noticed that his pillow had fallen off the bed onto the floor. It hadn't disturbed his sleep; his eyes remained closed, and his body remained motionless as I slowly crept toward him and picked up the pillow. And as I stood over his practically lifeless body, pillow in hand, I couldn't keep the thought from popping into my head: What if I just…*smothered* him?

Immediately, I began justifying it to myself. He was obviously suffering. He was going to die in five days anyway. I could kill him in his sleep and save him from all the fear, the dread, the anguish. It would be a mercy, wouldn't it?

"You don't think I could kill someone?" Lina had asked me, several vodka tonics deep. "No," I'd said. "Well, I can. And I have," she'd replied.

I had known she was lying. There are two kinds of people in the world: people who have killed other people and people who haven't. And once you've killed a person, it's pretty easy to tell who belongs in which category. I've killed three. Today, I almost killed a fourth.

I couldn't do it. I choked back a pathetic sob and shoved the pillow under his head. He didn't stir, and I turned and left, afraid that if I stayed with him long enough, I would change my mind.

—Mia

October 12, 2089
Day 43, year 12

Today, Joel opened his eyes and told me he was sorry.

"For what?" I asked.

"Everything," he answered.

He's gotten some of his strength back. Maybe, the knowledge that soon all the pain will be gone has given him a little energy. We even went for a slow walk around his neighborhood, not saying anything but stopping every now and then to listen to the birds singing and dragonflies humming around us. The sounds of nature. The sounds of life.

Three more days.

—Mia

October 14, 2089
Day 45, year 12

We went over the plan today.

Well technically, *I* went over the plan, and Joel just listened. His job is easy: take the medicine and fall asleep. I, on the other hand, am the one who has to follow all the pages of instructions to the letter because apparently, killing oneself isn't as simple as just swallowing pills and falling asleep. You have to do each step and adhere to the time line because if you don't, you could end up either dying in agony or not dying at all. It's supposed to feel just like falling asleep if you follow the directions exactly, although I don't know how anyone could possibly know that. Did the doctors who came up with these drugs use them to kill someone and then bring that person back to life and ask "So, how did that feel?"

I asked Joel if he wanted to do it in the morning or at night. He blinked a few times with wide, terrified eyes, and I wondered, after all this, if he'd even have the guts to go through with this tomorrow.

"I think night," he said eventually. "I want to spend the day with you."

"Doing what?"

"Doing nothing. Just being with you." He reached out and took my hand; his own hand was freezing cold. "I love you, Mia."

I jerked my hand back with a force that surprised both of us. "Don't do that," I demanded. "Don't *say* that!"

"But, Mia, I do. I love you."

"Well, I don't love you," I spat out. There had always been a tiny part of me that protested when I insisted that I didn't love him, a tiny shard of my heart that whispered, "No, don't throw it away, forgive him, admit that there is no horrible thing he could ever do to you that would change how you truly feel about him." But this time, this time, I meant it.

I don't love him. And I feel free.

We stared at each other in silence before he slowly reached up to kiss me, and I let him. When he pulled away, he had tears streaming down his face. "I don't want you to love me," he said firmly. "I don't deserve it."

I locked my eyes with his. "What do you want from me then?" I asked coldly.

He buried his face in his hands. "I want you to forgive me," he answered.

Forgiveness. More than anything, more than love itself, forgiveness is what he wanted before he died. My brain formed the words; they slid down to the back of my throat, and finally, my mouth opened, and I let them out, "I forgive you, Joel."

I don't know if I meant it. I don't think it mattered in the moment. Tears flowed harder and faster from his eyes; *finally*, he was ugly crying. I gently dried his face, gently kissed his cheek, gently traced his collarbones with my fingers. He fell asleep in his bed, and I am lying next to him. I can't sleep. I'm watching the slow rise and fall of his chest, listening to the ragged breaths escaping his lips, waiting for the sun to rise and bring the day hurtling toward us, unprepared though we may be.

—Mia

October 15, 2089
Day 46, year 12

Like I said before, most days are completely unremarkable. You go to work, you eat, you sleep, you spend time with friends if you're lucky enough to have them. Our days are numbered now, quite literally: day twenty-five, day twenty-six, day twenty-seven, and on and on. It makes it hard to remember the days that stand out from the rest.

But today? Today is day forty-six, year 12. And today is remarkable.

I went out this morning while Joel was still sleeping and brought back a breakfast of frozen pizza and beer. It seemed an appropriate last meal. I had to keep an eye on the time because Joel couldn't eat or drink anything but clear liquid twelve hours before the procedure.

Procedure. That's a pretty mild way to describe suicide.

Anyway, we ate and drank and felt like the most important people in the world, and today, we were. And although we tried to hang on to each moment for as long as we possibly could, eventually, the food ran out and the alcohol had mostly all been drunk, and there was nothing left to say. We just sat in silence with the dirty dishes between us. Neither one of us wanted to be the one to address what was going to happen next.

I abruptly stood up and started picking up the plates slowly and painstakingly and putting them into the sink.

"What are you doing?" Joel asked.

"I'm cleaning your dishes."

"What the hell does it matter if the dishes are clean or not?"

"It *does* matter. It does." I scrubbed vigorously.

"Mia, stop. Just sit with me. Please."

A slippery glass suddenly leapt out of my unsteady hand and landed with a spectacular crash on the tiled floor. Joel didn't flinch. Angrily, I stomped over to the closet and grabbed a broom.

"You're going to cut your foot open," Joel casually observed.

I continued to get angry and let the anger fuel my determination to get every last piece of glass off of the floor. With much effort,

Joel lifted himself from his seat and grabbed my shoulders with as much strength as he could. "Mia, *stop!*"

I was done. I couldn't handle one more second of this. The broom clattered to the floor, and I sank to my knees and screamed into my hands. Joel joined me on the floor. "Shh, Mia, shh," he said gently, "It's okay. I mean, my god, I don't need you to clean my apartment. That's not why you're here."

I turned and gave him a look that I can only assume was filled with ice because he cautiously began to inch away from me. "You don't even understand how lucky you are, do you?" I hissed at him. "Nobody, *nobody* knows when their life is going to end! We all just walk around, day after day, alive for now but always terrified. One minute we're breathing, the next minute we're not. It's enough to make you go insane. But you? Well, you get to decide how, when, and where you die! No fear, no uncertainty, no going against your will. How? Comfortably in your sleep. When? After a nice two weeks spent trying to find closure. Where? In the comfort of your own home. But you know what? Your home looks like shit. It's disgusting. Your sheets are dirty. Your clothes are everywhere. You get to choose where to spend your final moments, and you're going to choose to spend them with *these*?" I shoved a dirty plate into his face. "So, yes, Joel. Yes. I *do* need to clean your apartment. I'm not going to let you die in filth."

And I stood. And I grabbed the remaining dishes, soaked them, and placed them in the dishwasher. And after a few moments, Joel appeared next to me at the sink, silently loading the dishwasher with dishes that would never come out again.

The rest of the day was a blur. We put on movies that neither of us watched. We made tea that neither of us drank. We sat on his couch, and with every hour that passed, we unconsciously moved closer to each other until I found myself in his arms. We drifted in and out of sleep. And then the alarm went off, unwelcome, terrifying and discomforting as an electric shock down my spine. We locked eyes. It was time. I helped him to his bed and gently wrapped his blankets around him. He kissed my cheek and leaned his head back onto the pillow.

I had read the instructions a dozen times over the past few days, not including the three additional times that I read it today, because I absolutely didn't want to get anything wrong. There were two separate medications. One was a sedative, a heavy one, to make sure he would be asleep for everything. The other one would shut down the rest of his body: his breathing would slow, his heart would stop beating, his eyes would never flicker again.

Take the sedative with a full glass of water. It should take full effect after thirty minutes. If it does not take effect after thirty minutes, an additional dose may be required.

I poured the water. I shook out two of the pills from the bottle. I carried them to his room. His eyes were closed, his breathing slow. He was preparing for it, whatever it would feel like. I helped him sit up. I told him that soon he would start to feel sleepy, and that was good because it meant the medicine was working. He swallowed the pills and grimaced. "They taste like shit," he said.

"I don't think you're supposed to taste them."

"Just give me a shot of vodka or something to wash it down."

"I don't think you're supposed to do that."

He angrily fell back onto his pillow and closed his eyes. "Just give me the damn alcohol, Mia. I want to go to sleep."

I rushed to help him sit back up. "You can't sleep! Not yet. You have to take the other one first."

Joel's face cracked into a sob. "I don't want to."

He looked so pathetic, so small, so scared. It made my stomach turn. "Don't do this, Joel. Please. You know this is the best thing for you to do."

"What if it's not? What if I have five more months left?"

"You don't, Joel. You have a few more weeks at best. And you would be in agony the whole time."

Joel's sobs turned into whimpers. "Don't, Mia. Please, don't make me do this."

I was doing everything in my power to stay calm, to stay rational, to stay reassuring. "I'm not making you do anything, Joel. You chose this. Remember? You chose this because it's what's best for you."

"Please, don't make me do this!" he cried again. He grabbed the collar of my sweater desperately, eyes wild and terrified.

I trembled but stood firm. "It's normal, it's normal to be afraid—"

"No! I'm not afraid. I'm just not ready!" he screamed. He tried to get up, but it was too late. The medicine was beginning to kick in. His eyelids began to flutter, his breathing slowed. "Mia," he whispered. "I'm not ready."

He wasn't ready. Neither was I. I wasn't ready to participate in yet another human being's death. "We're never ready," I said gently. "You won't be ready five weeks from now or five months or five years. And that's why I'm here. So we can be not ready together." My hands shook as I poured another glass of water from the pitcher by his bed. I held his hand until the next alarm went off. He was nearly unconscious.

"Joel," I whispered. "One more swallow, and that's it."

He opened his eyes for what would turn out to be the last time. "You're beautiful," he said, and for a moment, I remembered what it had felt like to love him.

"So are you," I replied. I held the water to his lips. "Ready?"

He swallowed the water. Then he swallowed the medicine. Then he swallowed the very last bit of water. "Yes," he answered.

And that was it.

It only took a few minutes. It was hard to even tell when exactly it happened. But eventually, his chest stopped moving, and everything was still. I swept a lock of sweaty hair from his forehead and kissed it. I stepped out of his apartment into the hallway, gently locking the door behind me. And when I finally made it back to my own apartment, I buried my face in my pillow and screamed.

Today is day forty-six, year 12.

Today is remarkable.

—Mia

October 19, 2089
Day 49, year 12

Haven't slept since Joel.
    Haven't eaten either.
    That's it. That's all.

—Mia

October 20, 2089
Day 50, year 12

One of the Jennifers from apartment C knocked on my door this afternoon. She came inside without an invitation and slowly paced around the room. Even before she spoke, I knew something terrible had happened. She told me that the other Jennifer had been arrested for not only possessing heroin but also dealing it.

"I had no idea she was *dealing*. No idea," she repeated over and over. "I'm clean! I've been clean for weeks. I thought she was trying to get clean too. We were gonna do it together, get clean in year 12."

"I'm so sorry," I said. What else could I have said?

Jennifer just sank to the floor in exhaustion. She hadn't been sleeping either. "She's gone. I have to go get her in a couple weeks. And she won't be the same." She looked up at me. "She's getting aged."

I nodded in response to this new information. I wasn't surprised. Heroin dealing would get her at least five years and maybe up to ten.

"I need you to tell me what to expect," Jennifer said.

I studied her eyes; they were tearful and desperate, the eyes of brokenhearted love. No one had been brokenhearted over my aging. I had traversed it alone. I joined Jennifer on the floor and gently put an arm around her.

"She *will* be the same," I reassured her, "just in a different body. She might be in some pain at first. You'll have to be patient with her. She'll feel self-conscious about her body and find all kinds of new faults with it. Love her anyway. Kiss the parts of her that have changed the most and tell her they are beautiful. She will tell you that you deserve someone better. Don't believe it. There *is* no one better. She's it. Stay with her till the minute she dies."

Jennifer shivered and I wrapped my arm around her tighter.

"And forgive her," I added.

A lump began to form in my throat as I remember Joel's desperate plea: *I want you to forgive me.* "Forgive her always. Forgive her when she resents you for being young. Forgive her when she demands too much of you. Forgive her when you can't do anything to make her happy. Just forgive her..." And then I felt the walls closing in, and the smell of Jennifer's shampoo suffocating me, and I abruptly stood and led her to the door.

"Thank you," she whispered as I closed the door in her face.

—Mia

October 27, 2089
Day 57, year 12

After the encounter with Jennifer, I had no more disturbances until yesterday morning when Jonah knocked on my door, and when I didn't answer, he unlocked it and came in. I was lying in my bed of blankets and shirts facing the wall.

"Mia." I could tell from the sound of his voice that he was scowling. "Mia, I thought you were dead."

Why aren't I dead? That's a good question. Why do I have to live when everyone I love has already gotten to die?

"I called you so many times. You never answered. Care to explain?"

I rolled over to see Jonah's angry face.

"Mia, say something, dammit!" he shouted.

I squeezed my eyes shut. "Please, leave me alone," I whispered.

"No. I'm not going anywhere. Are you sick? Do you need the hospital?"

The hospital.

When was the last time I went to the hospital?

"Joel died," I blurted out.

"Who's Joel?" asked Jonah.

I didn't answer. Who *was* Joel? Had he even really existed? Jonah's voice sounded like it was underwater. He started saying my name over and over, and each time, it sounded farther and farther away. I don't remember blacking out. I don't remember the ambulance taking me away. I don't remember them restarting my heart (they told me my heart stopped on the way to the hospital). I woke up in a hospital bed with tubes in my hands and Jonah sitting in the corner of the room eating something that smelled horrible. He didn't say anything when I opened my eyes, but he slowly stood up, walked over to my bed, and placed my journal by my feet. Then he gathered his things and left.

—Mia

November 1, 2089
Day 63, year 12

Still here.

"You're doing much better," the doctors say. But when I ask them when I can go home, they tell me "It's difficult to say for sure" and then awkwardly leave the room.

Jonah has visited a few times. He never talks to me, just sits in the corner and eats greasy fast food and then leaves. But his company is nice. It's the only company I ever get.

I haven't been writing much. I don't have anything to say. I'm just so, so tired. I want to fall asleep again and not wake up.

—Mia

November 3, 2089
Day 65, year 12

"I demand to go home," I told Jonah yesterday.

He just laughed and finished swallowing a bite of whatever foul-smelling thing he was eating. "Really? You demand it?"

"Yes. I'm feeling better. I can eat and drink and stand on my own."

"You're practically suicidal."

"I'm not anymore. I don't belong here."

And we went back and forth like that until a doctor came into my room, and in the end, I won. I was deemed well enough to go home. So here I am. Apartment D again.

The first thing I did when I got here was collapse into my pile of clothes on the floor and roll around while laughing with insanity. I was like an animal marking its scent. I wanted to grab everything and call it all *mine*.

Then last night, I went down to Jonah's. He frowned when he saw me but didn't protest as I forced my way in. "You seem happy," he said.

"I am," I replied with a smile.

"Have you eaten?"

"No."

"Are you hungry?"

"Yes." And a plate of sausages and greasy potatoes appeared in front of me.

We enjoyed a drink after dinner, several drinks actually. Empty bottles sat in piles in every corner of the room. I was drunk and giddy and just happy to be in somebody else's company. Jonah told dirty jokes, and I laughed. I told him all about Joel, and it surprisingly didn't hurt. It felt satisfying and comforting, like talking about your favorite book to someone who's never read it before.

Then I started to feel dizzy. I told Jonah it was from the alcohol even though I knew it wasn't. I asked him to help me home. He rolled his eyes but agreed. We had just gotten to my door, and I was fumbling to open it when I heard a different door creak open behind me. Apartment C.

I turned around and saw Lina standing in front of the open door, makeup smeared all over her face and a tiny tank top barely covering what little breasts she had. She was barefoot and carrying most of her clothes in her arms. She was a little startled when she saw me, but only for a second, because then she licked her lips and smiled at me. She walked away, revealing a disheveled Jennifer cowering in the doorway. We locked eyes. Neither of us said a word. We didn't have to. Every fiber of her being screamed at me, "*I'm sorry.*" And I could only reply, "*me too.*"

—Mia

November 4, 2089
Day 66, year 12

I think the end is near. And if you think I'm being dramatic, you should know that I fell in the shower this morning because my head was spinning so badly. I think my ankle is either sprained or broken, but I'm not going back to the hospital. Not yet. The next time I go to the hospital, I don't think I'll ever leave.

Day 150. I'm supposed to make it to day 150. That's what the doctor said. What's the math? Day 150 minus day 66…that's 84 days. Twelve weeks. Three months. Honestly, it seems like forever.

At least the pain isn't so bad. They gave me pills for pain management, enough pills to last for a few months. That's pretty irresponsible of them now that I think of it. Who would stop me from swallowing them all at once and getting it over with? Not that anybody cares about a convicted murderer killing themselves.

The dizziness though…the dizziness is so much worse than the pain. Everything spins and tilts sideways and upside down. I'm in constant motion while staying completely still. Every now and then, for a few moments, I'll get some relief, and I'll write and have a drink of water and use the bathroom. I won't eat anything because I'll throw it up immediately once the room starts spinning again. I don't remember the last thing I ate. Was it the sausage and potatoes at Jonah's place? It has to be, there's no food in my kitchen…sausage and potatoes, and now I'm feeling sick again, and the room is about to start spinning…

—Mia

November 6, 2089
Day 68, year 12

Sideways
A poem by Mia Einecle

When the world goes sideways, I just close my eyes,
And I picture it all the right way in my head.
And no matter how much it spins, spins, spins on the outside
on the inside, it is still.
It is quiet.
It is calm.
So I keep my eyelids sealed like the doors to a padded cell,
a soft white tomb for my eyes.
And while the world outside stays sideways,
~~on the inside, I am still.~~
~~on the inside, I am motionless.~~

I don't know how to end it. I like the word "motionless," but it doesn't really fit. "Still" fits better, but I already used it earlier.
What if I switched them?

And no matter how much it spins, spins, spins on the outside
on the inside, it is motionless.

And while the world outside stays sideways,
on the inside, I am still.

Eh.
Is there another word for "motionless"?
Frozen? Would "frozen" work?

And while the world outside stays sideways,
on the inside, I am frozen.

No. It's garbage. *I'm* garbage. I'm losing my head. By next week, I might not be able to put a full sentence together.

This can't be it. This can't be how I spend my final days—alone and lying in a pile of dirty clothes on the floor.

The other Jennifer came home yesterday. I alternated between violently puking into my backpack and staying very, very quiet so I could listen in on their conversation. I had been exposed to many of the Jennifers' fights before. They never seemed to care if they were being heard by anyone else or not. Yesterday was different. They spoke quietly and calmly, and even with the paper-thin walls in this building, I could barely hear them. That was the first bad sign. Quiet arguing means that it's over. When you yell and scream, it means that you still care, that you are desperate to keep things from falling apart and so you flail around like an animal in a trap frantically trying to survive at all costs.

I remember the last fight Joel and I had. I stayed calm the whole time. He screamed and cried, begged me not to quit treatment. I quietly told him to leave. I didn't shed a tear. If I had yelled back at him, things would have been different, except no, not really. He would still be dead. I would still be alone.

It took a few hours before it was over. Finally, I heard a door open and close and the other Jennifer's heavy footsteps tread down the hallway, getting fainter and fainter until I couldn't hear them at all. The first Jennifer stayed behind. I could hear her sobbing. They were quiet sobs, not big ugly sobs like mine always were. They were the beautiful kind of sobs that would make her eyes big and shiny and would leave tear tracks down her perfectly pink cheeks that would twinkle when the light hit them just right.

Jennifer, you are the worst kind of person. I would say I hope you and Lina are happy together, but you don't deserve Lina, and Lina doesn't deserve you. Neither of you deserve anyone's love. I hope Lina sends you out her door and that the next heavy footsteps I hear leaving this wretched building are yours. I hope that you start ugly crying all the way out the front door and into the street and that everyone who sees you gives you an awkward glance and then quickly looks away and not a single person stops to ask you what's wrong.

—Mia

November 10, 2089
Day 72, year 12

I've got it! I think.

When the world goes sideways, I just close my eyes,
And I picture it all the right way in my head.
And no matter how much it spins, spins, spins on the outside,
on the inside everything is frozen in place and moments last forever.
So I keep my eyelids sealed like the doors to a padded cell,
a soft white tomb for my eyes.
And while the world outside stays sideways,
on the inside, I am as still as time continues to be.

It needs some work. But it's better. Maybe my head has a few more lines of prose left in it after all.

Jonah has been coming by to check on me. He stopped by for the first time yesterday morning and again last night, and he just left after spending this morning with me. He brings me sparkling water to drink and tells me to drink it slowly. It has a funny taste. Jonah says he crushes up vitamins in it. I can't keep food down and I need nutrients, he says. I humor him and drink the fizzy bitter water, and it makes my nose itch, but I never feel like throwing up after.

I think Jonah might be the only person on the planet who will actually miss me when I'm dead. He's my only friend. I haven't spoken with my family in almost a year. They might think I'm dead already.

I've started to think about what I want to happen to my body… afterward, I mean. I'll be cremated. I doubt any part of my body is suitable to be donated to anyone. So I'll just be a pile of ashes locked in a box. It makes my heart race just thinking about it. I can't stay locked in a box for all eternity. I need Jonah to do something with me. I think I want him to scatter me all over the tree I saw out my window on the day that I woke up. That tree weirdly gave me hope. I wonder how many other people have woken up in that room terrified, and then they look out the window at that tree and suddenly life seems possible again. I want to be a part of that. I want to give hope to people like me.

—Mia

November 11, 2089
Day 73, year 12

I told Jonah today about what I wanted him to do with my ashes. I don't think he really knew how to react while I was talking, but after I was done, he nodded and said, "That sounds nice." And I just looked at him for a while, comforted by his familiar ugliness. And I remembered all the little kindnesses he's shown me this past year. And I thought about how, in his own Jonah-like way, he did truly love me, and there weren't many other people who could say the same. And felt the urge to hug him even though I knew he hadn't bathed yet and probably smelled like burnt grease. And then I started to cry. But it wasn't an ugly cry. I cried soft, quiet tears down my cheeks, just like Joel used to do, and then I started laughing like a maniac. I've finally figured out how to look beautiful while crying.

Jonah stood up and abruptly interrupted my emotions. "Come with me," he said.

"What for?"

"Just come. Don't ask questions."

And so I followed him back to his apartment, and when he opened the door, I shrieked in surprise. The place was spotless. The floor had been vacuumed. There were no greasy dishes in the sink. The bathroom had been scrubbed. I had always thought the sink and shower and toilet were tan, but no, they're actually *white*. Sparkling white. Jonah took my hand and pulled me into the bedroom. His old chair was gone. The piles of trash and empty bottles were gone. The only things in the room were a big bed with plush white blankets, a small bedside table, and two beautiful lamps that cast a relaxing light over everything. I couldn't get over how good it looked and, more importantly, how good it *smelled*.

"Jonah, this looks amazing!" I said. "I'm so happy for you!"

And then I did actually hug him, and to my surprise, he smelled nice too. It was like every grease molecule surrounding Jonah's existence had been pulverized. He awkwardly hugged me back, and when I pulled away, he had the slightest curve of a smile around his mouth.

"I did it for you," he said sheepishly. Jonah had never ever cleaned his place before inviting me over.

I eyed him suspiciously. "Is this some sort of bribe?" I teased him.

But Jonah's face remained serious. "I guess you can think of it that way," he answered. He gently put his hand on my arm; again, something he had never done before. "I want you to move back in with me."

I jerked my arm away and playfully shoved him. "No, you don't," I replied. "Why would you want me taking over your couch?"

"I don't want you on the couch. I want you to stay in my room."

I understood immediately what he meant.

He meant that he knew I didn't have much time left. He knew I had no one around to be with me. He wasn't going to let me die alone in an empty apartment. He would give me his bed. And he would give me his company.

I started crying again—this time, it was an ugly cry—and threw my arms around him. We're about the same height, Jonah and me, so my face was buried pretty comfortably in his shoulder, and he just let me stand there getting my tears and snot all over his jacket while he gently stroked my hair.

"Come on," he finally whispered. "Let's go get your stuff."

I'm in Jonah's bed now, *my* bed, with the plush white blankets and pillows. I'm so comfortable that I don't want to fall asleep because then I won't get to feel how comfortable I am. Jonah has relocated himself to the living room. My clothes are all being washed. Dinner is being made and will be brought to me on a tray. I feel like royalty.

This is where I will be spending the last bit of my life. Jonah has hired a nurse from the hospital to come take care of me. She's going to come by once a day just to check on me and then move in once I start to…decline, I guess is the word. I didn't ask, but I know Jonah is paying for everything. I still don't know what I did to deserve all this kindness.

I don't quite know how I feel about death right now. It feels like this abstract, hypothetical thing, not like an inevitability that could come knocking on my door any day. I'm not exactly scared of death, but I'm not ready for it either. I actually used to think about it a lot. I know it sounds morbid. But your mind goes to weird places when you're high. I would smoke with Elliot, and we'd lay in the grass on our backs, staring up at the sky, and it was all just so infinite and sad, and I felt infinite and sad and also really wise somehow. And so we'd start talking about heaven and whether or not it exists and how to get there if it does. And then we'd wonder what heaven was even like because maybe we wouldn't want to go there if it was just a bunch of angels and clouds and golden streets and people playing harps.

I never felt scared. Death is far enough away when you're sixteen that you can talk about it without it seeming inevitable. I'll never know for sure, but I assume that at some point in your life, maybe in your fifties or sixties, something switches in your brain, and all of a sudden, death stops being hypothetical, and it turns into a real concrete thing that follows you around and makes you do things like get life insurance and create a will and stop drinking so much alcohol. And even though it gets closer every day, you don't mind it so much because you're so used to it being there, and when you really stop to consider it, it actually does make you appreciate your life more. I wish death felt real to me. As close as it is, it still feels just as far away as it did when I would get high and look up at the sky and think about the clouds in heaven that you could somehow sit on without falling through them. But that switch in my brain never got the chance to flip.

—Mia

November 13, 2089
Day 75, year 12

Now that I'm dying, I have something that I need to confess.

Deep down, I never knew for sure if I was really a murderer or not. There was always a part of me, no matter what the police said or the lawyers said or the judge and jury said, that wasn't entirely convinced that I had the heart of a cold-blooded killer. But now I know for sure that I do.

The nurse that Jonah hired has started to visit me. Her first visit was yesterday. She didn't examine me. She just asked me a bunch of questions and wrote down my answers. She has blue eyes. I've never met a person with eyes as blue as hers. They're very soothing. So is her voice. And her smell. And the way her pen looks when she holds it in her delicate hand. And the sound it makes—"scratch, scratch, scratch"—while she scribbles notes in her notepad. I think I might have fallen asleep while she was still in the room. I don't remember her leaving.

She came again today and sat at the foot of my bed. Her blue eyes were serious, her delicate hands were clasped together, her voice sounded uncertain. "I'm not supposed to tell you this," she said, "but I really think you should know."

I sat up as best as I could and waited for her to keep talking. She stared at the wall and wouldn't meet my gaze.

"This is confidential information. If anyone finds out that I told you this, I'll get fired, maybe even aged. Understand?"

My heart started pounding. "I won't say anything," I assured her. And then she took a deep breath.

"On day 276, year 11, your mother, Athena Einecle, gave birth to a baby boy. There were complications. Your mother survived, but the baby was born with irreparable brain damage. He fought for weeks. It just wasn't enough. He passed away earlier this morning." Finally, she looked me in the eye. "He looked just like you."

There were no tears, no sadness in her voice. Her demeanor made it obvious that she had seen plenty of babies die before and broken the news to bereaved families of all kinds. She had mastered the art of simultaneously portraying sympathy and maintaining professionalism.

"Thank you for telling me," was all I said before she got up and left.

This is my confession.

This is how I know I'm a murderer.

I feel happy.

So, so incredibly happy.

I'm happy the kid died because he never asked to be born. He never had a say in whether or not he wanted to be my replacement, a "second chance," as my mother had put it. He would have never been his own person. His entire existence would have been my mother's consolation prize, a peg being constantly squeezed into the giant ugly hole that I had left behind. And I'm happy my mother survived because now she can live as long as she wants and she will never have another kid ever, and I hope it hurts like hell. I hope she lives every second of her life in agony, and I hope she lives a long time.

—Mia

November 16, 2089
Day 78, year 12

The Attic
A poem by Mia Einecle

I have regrets.
But I carry them well.
I collect cares and climb stairs
and hide them far away.
I won't think of them again, those secret affairs.
They will stay where I place them
because they can't walk through walls
and they don't have keys.
Time is more than medicine on my terms.
And I keep it all on my terms.

Yesterday, Jonah sat with me in my room and asked me if I had any regrets. "I'm not talking about the obvious stuff, like killing those boys," he clarified. "I mean something like, is there something you wish you would have told someone but never did? Or do you wish you would have traveled somewhere? Or do you wish that you had never gotten to know Joel?"

The last option made me glare at him sharply. "I don't regret Joel," I said firmly. "I don't regret anything about us." I gazed wistfully at the drawing of my face that Joel had given me which I now have displayed on my bedside table. There's no point in keeping it hidden anymore.

"I had a Joel once," Jonah said, and a wistful smile played around the corners of his mouth. "His name was James." He leaned back in his chair with a surprising amount of confidence for someone his size. The chair creaked in protest. "That was a long time ago though."

I studied Jonah. His ugliness had shocked me when I first met him; now it's familiar and comforting. I tried to imagine him younger, lighter, not yet jaded by the world around him. I tried to imagine what he would look like as a beautiful person. "Tell me about James," I finally said.

Legally, Jonah and I are the same age. In reality, he's lived thirty years longer than I have. I was in kindergarten when the New Age began; Jonah was in his midthirties. He has memories, vivid memories, of life from the Old Age. He was twenty-seven, he told me, when he met James.

James was a twenty-year-old singer with bright eyes and youthful naivety to match them. He was exciting while Jonah was quiet, confident while Jonah was nervous, yet to be scathed while Jonah already bore several of life's scars. James performed in nightclubs and bars all over the city and quickly became a local celebrity. His voice, Jonah told me, was like brand-new glass.

"No scratches. No cracks. Just…effortless pure tone. Magical." Jonah's eyes began to twinkle. He sat six feet away from me, but he might as well have been on the other side of the world. Slowly, as if he were retelling a dream, he described their chance meeting at a bar one night.

"It was after ten o'clock. I had just finished a shift at the restaurant where I worked. I needed a drink. There was a bar right by the restaurant where some of us would go after our shifts were finished. We'd usually all wait for each other and go together. Not that night though. That night, I was by myself. It was Christmas Eve. Everyone else had plans."

I remember Christmas Eve.

Dad baked pies and cookies. It rained. I was four years old. Mom wore a red silk robe all day and watched movies with me on the couch, and when I tried to get up, she would grab me tightly by the wrist and pull me back down and I would cry. She had a glass that she kept filling with something that looked like plain water but made me wrinkle my nose when I smelled it, and the more she drank, the smellier she got. After a while, Dad came and took me away from her. She didn't protest. She was barely conscious.

"Mommy isn't feeling very well today," Dad whispered as he led me to the kitchen. "Come look at all the treats I made for you!" And he poured me a glass of milk and set a plate of unfrosted cookies in front of me that were shaped like pine trees, and we took turns covering them in green icing and dunking them in our milk. I was happy.

Dad was trying his best to be happy. He kept a smile on his face and playfulness in his voice. But even as a four-year-old, I saw past it. His eyes were too sad. But, God bless him, he made it a good day for me. I don't know if he loved me all the time, but he loved me that day, and he loved me over the next several days while Mom stayed motionless on the couch with her movies, only moving to make a trip to the bathroom. Sometimes, it sounded like she was crying in there. Other times, it sounded like she was moaning in pain. I would be scared, and I would cling to Dad's arm, and he would just rub my back and tell me not to worry; Mommy just wasn't feeling very well still. Every time, after a few minutes, the toilet would flush, the sink would run, and Mom would come out looking like a walking corpse and plant herself back on the couch. Dad would get up and peer into the bathroom. Usually, he would come right back to me, but a few times, he frowned and knelt down to wipe something up off the floor.

One time, he wasn't there. Mom had gotten up to use the bathroom. She made all the usual frightening noises, and I covered my ears with my hands to muffle them. The toilet flushed, the sink ran, and Mom came back out looking like the same zombie she had been before. Fear turned into curiosity. What was wrong in the bathroom? Was there a monster in there? I would find out! I tiptoed to the door and slid it open. There was a smell that I didn't recognize, not a normal bathroom smell. It was meaty, fishy—I don't know how else to describe it. It smelled the way you would expect a dead deer on the highway to smell. And then I saw the blood. It wasn't a lot, just a few drops on the toilet seat and a faint line running down from the seat to the floor. Curiosity turned right back into fear, and I started crying for Dad. He came almost immediately. He looked upset. He quickly picked me up, carried me out of the bathroom, and closed the door.

"Is Mommy dying?" I whimpered. "I think Mommy is dying!"

And Dad just shook his head. "I told you before, MiMi," he said, and it was one of the few times that either of my parents had used an endearing nickname for me, "Mommy isn't feeling well. We need to be very good and very patient."

"For how long?" I asked.

He sighed and closed his eyes. "A couple more days, I think," he answered. "It should all be over in a couple days."

And he was right. A few days later, Mom was walking around the house in normal clothes. There was no more crying or moaning. The bathroom stayed clean. The air smelled fresh. It was like nothing out of the ordinary had ever happened. So I simply pushed everything out of my head and began to look forward to the next Christmas. But there never was a next Christmas.

Man, I got off track there for a little bit. I was talking about Jonah and James and how they met on Christmas Eve. James was singing and strumming a guitar when Jonah saw him for the first time. Jonah became very aware of himself in that moment: how he sat, how he held his drink, how his work clothes smelled like garlic. He admired James from a distance but would have never approached him. Fortunately for Jonah, James was not so shy. He finished his set and walked right up to Jonah and sat down on a vacant barstool.

"You look lonely, friend," James said with a smile. Those were his exact words according to Jonah: "You look lonely, friend." He asked the bartender for a glass of water.

"Nothing stronger?" Jonah asked him. No, James had replied. He had been sober for six months. "Good for you," Jonah had said. "I couldn't do that. I've tried." He knocked back the rest of his drink for emphasis.

James just kept smiling. "I had a lot of support," he said. "Especially from my girlfriend."

Yes, the handsome, young, bright-eyed singer was in a committed relationship. With a woman. So that was it, Jonah had figured. Disappointing, but not an unusual experience for a gay man.

Except that Jonah kept seeing James performing at different bars all around the city with his beat-up guitar and glassy voice. Jonah never purposely looked for him, he just seemed to appear. Sometimes, he would simply give Jonah a smile of recognition between songs and go back to playing his songs; other times, he would take a thirty-minute break and hop down off the stage just so they could sit together and talk and drink nonalcoholic beverages together. Sometimes, James brought friends along. Sometimes, he even brought Anna, his girlfriend. She was lovely and delightful and clearly adored James, and James was very good at pretending to adore her too. Of all of James's friends, only Jonah noticed the slightly uncomfortable way he held her on his lap or the half-second glances he would give to the male bartender with the tattoos while he poured drinks and cleaned glasses and chatted with customers. Only Jonah knew that beneath those bright eyes and relentless smile was a different boy entirely, a boy who had never seen the light of day but was desperately pleading for his life.

It happened quickly and unceremoniously. Jonah was leaving after one too many beers, and James offered to go with him to make sure he got home safely. It was an obvious excuse even to their densest of friends. While Jonah was only about half his current body weight back then, he was still perfectly capable of keeping himself from danger. Anna gave him a strange look but said nothing.

"She knew," Jonah said. "She knew deep down. You can only hide who you truly are for so long."

The two men walked slowly and most certainly made an interesting sight: an innocent-looking youth, skinny and perfectly sober, attempting to keep a hairy barrel-chested man, drunk off his ass, from falling. When they got back to Jonah's place, James took over, making coffee and gathering blankets with the familiarity of someone who had been there dozens of times before. It started with a single kiss on the lips. It ended with awkward sex at the foot of the bed and tears pouring from James's eyes as he begged Jonah not to say anything to anyone.

"That's the gay life," Jonah sighed as he continued to tell the story. "I'm an ugly bastard now. Back in the '60s though...that was a different story. I wasn't the prettiest guy in town, but I was okay enough to be the secret guilty pleasure of straight men who always begged afterward, 'Please, don't tell my wife, my girlfriend, my fiancée.' If that was my role in society, I had accepted it. But then there was James…" Jonah's twinkling eyes turned sour. He still wouldn't make eye contact. "I couldn't let go of James."

What followed, Jonah said, was two and a half years that oscillated between sheer bliss and pure torture. James would shower Jonah with affection, gifts, exotic vacations. He told Jonah that he had never been happier. He thanked Jonah for helping him realize who he truly was. But James's happy, naive exterior wasn't enough to mask his inner turmoil. As time went on, he would lash out at Jonah for the most insignificant things, berate Jonah for his drinking even if it was just a single beer, blame Jonah for the fact that he hadn't gotten a gig in months because his old bridges with his music friends had been burned when he cheated on Anna. Then he would tearfully apologize, Jonah would forgive him, they would have passionate make-up sex, and the next day would be blissful again. The bliss would last for a day, maybe two, before James found something else to get angry about. Jonah would take the screaming and simply absorb it without giving any of it in return.

"I hate you!" James screamed at him one particularly volatile night.

"No, you don't," Jonah answered quietly. "You just hate yourself."

"That's the problem with being twenty-one, twenty-two," Jonah said to me. "Your existence blends so strongly with others that you can't even tell where you stop and the world begins. The things you hate in others are the things you hate in yourself. He hated my drinking because I knew my limitations and he didn't know his. He hated how calm I always was with him because he couldn't control his own emotions, and he took my stoicism as arrogance when it was simply me acknowledging that one of us had to be an adult about things. He wanted me to get angry, to fight, to threaten. He thought that was the sign of true love. He thought that staying calm meant apathy. And you know what? Maybe, he was right."

I remembered the Jennifers and how their relationship transitioned from shouting matches to quiet crying sessions. I remembered how numb I felt when Joel begged, begged, begged me not to quit treatment with tears in his eyes, and I had just stared at him and given him nothing.

"How did it end?" I asked.

Jonah just sighed and shook his head. "He left," he said. "One day, I came home from work. He had taken his things. He had taken some things we had bought together. He hadn't left so much as a message to explain. I was in shock, and I called him and messaged him. He never replied."

And finally, finally, I saw a single tear roll down Jonah's face. He didn't even seem to notice. "That was 2072. I remember it happened during the Summer Olympics. Do you remember the Olympics, Mia? The last one was in 2076. You were probably still in diapers back then. But…2072. I'll never forget that summer. Seventeen years ago. I've never been in love since."

His last sentence was the one that struck me the most. For as long as I've been alive, Jonah has been alone. And I looked at Jonah as he awkwardly tried to get comfortable in a chair that hadn't been designed for his body, and I sobbed at what a horrible friend I had been.

Jonah isn't ugly. He's big and hairy and sweaty, and he has dry skin that sheds obvious white flakes whenever he wears a black shirt, and he has unremarkable eyes that transform into starlight when he talks about the boy he fell in love with twenty years ago. And I love him.

I had always wanted a brother. That Christmas Eve when I was four was the closest I had ever gotten to having my wish come true, and it ended with blood on the toilet seat.

Jonah is my brother, I realized today. He watches out for me, he calls me out on my shit, he shows up when I hit rock bottom and have no one else to dig me out. And if I had never lost my friends or killed those boys or been aged and disowned by my biological family, I would have never met him.

I'm imagining two giant hands. One holds my family and my friends and Elliot and my life as a high school senior and the faint possibility of becoming a writer when I grow up. The other holds the Jennifers and apartment D and Kyle who always shares his weed with me and Joel, and on top of them all sits Jonah. If I could go back to last year and see the two paths in front of me, which one would I choose?

My answer is simple and childish: I want both. I want Matty and Juniper and Jorge and Elliot and Joel and Jonah, and maybe even Lina, just for the hell of it. I want them all. And that's the worst part about being a human being: our bodies can only be in one place at a time while our hearts want to be everywhere all at once.

—Mia

November 18, 2089
Day 80, year 12

My nurse told me her name today. It's Rose. I told her I thought it was a beautiful name.

Rose splits her work between the hospital and the aging facility. From how experienced she seems, I was surprised to learn that she's only twenty-six. She had been a prodigy in medical school, she said, graduating with her medical license at twenty-three. She had always been fascinated by the science of aging, so when the aging lab jumped at the chance to offer her a job, it was a dream come true. But, she said, she also loved working with patients in the hospital, and in the end, she worked out a deal where she could do both because it turns out that when you're really, *really* good at something, you can pretty much ask for whatever you want and you'll get it.

"So how did you end up with me?" I asked as she inserted my IV. She hadn't been lying when she said she was good. I literally didn't feel a thing.

She smiled at me. "I took some time off from the hospital," she said. "Jonah had sent out an advertisement to the hospitals in the area, looking for someone who could be a live-in nurse for his friend. It was something I had never done before, and I was interested. When I dug deeper and I found out who you were, I knew I had to do it. I had to meet you. And I'm so glad I did." She hung up a bag of fluid and removed her gloves. "I'm going to be honest with you, Mia, and I think you already know this," she said. "The next few days are not about making you well. I'm afraid that isn't possible. My job is to make you as comfortable as possible. You shouldn't be in any pain. If I do my job right, and I always do, then it will feel just like falling asleep…when the time comes." I felt her hand rest gently on my ankle.

"I will be moving in tomorrow. Jonah already has a bed set up for me in the living room. It'll be a tight fit, the three of us living here, but we'll make it work." She smiled again. She smiles an awful lot for someone who's constantly surrounded by dying people. "Get some rest now. I'll be back to check on you in about an hour, and if all is well, then I'll go finish packing and be back tomorrow for good."

I feel so good right now, it's insane. The best weed in the world doesn't compare to whatever drugs are being pumped into my arm. My head doesn't hurt. I'm not dizzy. I'm not nauseated. I barely even feel like I have a body, if that makes sense. If you've ever been in excruciating pain and then the pain stopped, you'll know what I mean. You really only notice your body when there's something wrong with it.

I'm getting sleepy now. I'll write more later.

—Mia

November 19, 2089
Day 81, year 12

Rose moved in today. She was here when I woke up this morning. I'm using the term "morning" liberally because I didn't open my eyes until noon.

I am now officially bedridden. I have to shit into a plastic bag that Rose empties out for me. I'm not even self-conscious about it. Dying makes you not care about shitting into a bag.

Jonah comes in a couple times a day. If I'm up for conversation, he'll stay. If not, he'll leave. He's easy like that.

I've been sleeping over sixteen hours a day for the past few days, mostly because I have literally nothing else to do. Watching movies hurts my eyes. Talking for too long makes me run out of breath. So I sleep and I write in here. Writing is taking longer now. My thoughts are all jumbled up and slow and uninteresting.

I started hearing music last night. It wasn't real music. It was just four notes that kept repeating over and over and over: a sort of high pitch, then a slightly lower pitch, then a much lower pitch, then a slightly higher pitch. I can hear it now as I'm writing this. I asked Rose and Jonah if they heard it. They didn't. I'm not surprised. The notes are all in my head because even when I plug my ears, I can still hear them plain as day.

"Hallucinations are common," Rose assured me. "They are perfectly harmless. Some might be a little frightening, but you are completely safe. I promise."

I'm safe.

I can sing it in my head along with the music. *I'm safe, I'm safe, I'm safe, I'm safe.*

—Mia

November 21, 2089
Day 83, year 12

I can honestly say nothing shocks me anymore. This past year, I have:

1. murdered three people and assisted in the suicide of a fourth;
2. lost my four best friends all in the same night;
3. had thirty years of my life erased from existence;
4. watched the beheadings of two different men, one of whom I knew personally;
5. fell in love, only to have that person leave me when I decided not to continue cancer treatment and then, when I changed my mind and tried treatment again, it didn't work;
6. met the brother of one the boys I murdered on a dating site and was nearly beaten to death; and
7. found out that my mother, who is now technically the same age as I am, got pregnant, gave birth, and then watched the kid die for five months.

Am I missing anything? How about the girl who took my old job, got me drunk, and had her way with me? Or the fact that my best friend in the whole world now is a hairy, sweaty, middle-aged gay man who never spoke more than three sentences in a row to me before I started dying? Or way back when I watched a little girl try to strangle her sister right in front of me and I had to scream for their father to run ass-naked out of the shower to split them up?

You've read this far. At this point, I doubt anything shocks you either.

I'm prefacing with all this because I actually do think the next thing I'm going to write will, in fact, shock you. It sure as hell shocked me.

My dad came to visit me today.

My actual, real-life dad.

There was a knock at my bedroom door this afternoon, and Rose popped her head in. "You have a visitor," she said. Considering

I can basically count the people I know who were still alive on one hand and two of them were already in the apartment, I was naturally curious.

"Okay," I replied.

It was only after he walked in and sat in the chair at the foot of my bed that I realized that it had been over a year since I had seen him last. He looked like he's aged a decade. He's forty-seven, just like me and Mom and Jonah, but he could have been sixty. His hair was almost completely white. He had lost thirty pounds at least; his clothes drooped and sagged off of his body and made him look like a walking weight-loss advertisement. He had wrinkles. Dad had never had wrinkles before. But despite all this, I recognized him instantly.

My dad.

"Wow," I said in disbelief. I had no other words than that, so I said it again a little quieter to myself, "Wow."

He stood and moved his chair closer to me. "MiMi. It's Dad," he felt the need to clarify for some reason.

"Yeah, I know. You haven't changed a bit," I lied.

He reached out to take my hand. I didn't protest. "You look so beautiful," he said. "You look just like your mother. It's amazing."

I jerked my hand away. I had never looked like my mother. She always made it a point to tell me so. She was small and delicate and graceful; I was bulky and awkward and had my dad's sharp German facial structure. I wasn't beautiful.

"You really do, you know," Dad said like he could read my thoughts, and then he broke down crying. "I just can't believe it. My Mia. I thought I'd never see you again."

"I've been here for a year, Dad," I said sharply. "I haven't left. You could have found me anytime."

"I know, I know!" he cried. "It was just—"

"Mom," I finished for him. I spit her name out like a cobra spits venom.

We watched a video once in Mr. Fuller's class about spitting cobras. I mean, that wasn't what the *whole* video was about. It was about poisonous reptiles and the effect of their poison on the human body. But the spitting cobra part was the only part that I really remembered after it was finished.

Dad looked sad. I felt no sympathy, at least not at first. "Your mother," he said, and his entire body looked like one giant sigh that had been held in for far too long, "your mother isn't well. She's really never been well. Not when we met in high school, not when we started dating, not when we married, not when we had you. She got worse after we had you. But it wasn't your fault. She just…she's sick. I think she was born sick." He stopped and waited, wondering if maybe I had something to say. I gave him stony silence.

He continued, "We were so young when we got married," he said. "Twenty years old. It should be illegal, honestly." He chuckled. I didn't. "We thought we were ready. We thought we were different than everyone else. We could handle marriage. We could handle family. We started trying immediately. After two years and four miscarriages, I finally convinced her to see someone. She was in denial, delusional even. She thought it was normal. Babies take time, she would tell me. That's why we had started trying so early. But I knew. I knew something was wrong.

"We went to a specialist. We were both tested. My test results were normal. Your mother's weren't. Her uterus was extremely abnormally shaped. It looked like it had never fully developed. Pregnancy would not only be extremely unlikely, it would be dangerous for both her and the baby. We left that day, and I cried. But your mother…she didn't shed a tear. She was ready to keep trying. She wouldn't take no for an answer. I was scared for her. I didn't want her to get pregnant. I didn't want to lose her. Sometimes I would…*fake* it…you know?"

I knew. You can add "listening to my dad discuss his ejaculation habits with my mother" to the list of things that don't shock me about this year.

"It was a blur, those next eight years. Miscarriages. Hospital visits. Then she just didn't get pregnant at all for several years. And then… there was you. We waited a month, two months, three months. And you weren't going anywhere." He smiled, and I softened. "It's crazy to think about. You should have never existed, Mia. But my god, I'm so happy you do." And then he gently held my forearm in both of his hands, and I could tell he meant it. "I love you, Mia," he said firmly. "I didn't say it enough when you were a kid. But I felt it every second of my life after you were born. I want you to know that."

As much as I tried to prevent it, my eyes grew misty. "I love you too, Dad," I said. "And I'm so sorry about the baby."

He let his tears fall carelessly down his face, preferring to hold onto me instead of wiping them away. "We named him Elliot Jorge Matthew Einecle," he said. "Your mother didn't want to. But I insisted." His tears flowed faster. So did mine. "I loved those boys just like you did, Mia. I loved Juniper too. I never told you that, I know. Sometimes, when they would all come over to the house, I would imagine what it would be like to have a house full of kids like that. And when everyone was preoccupied, I would sneak off to my office, lock the door, and let myself sob as hard as I needed to. Sometimes, it only took a few minutes. Sometimes, it took the rest of the day."

And suddenly, Dad couldn't talk anymore, and he stood up and began pacing the room. And I started remembering Dad a little clearer: how he would quietly set out snacks whenever the gang would come over because my mother wouldn't do it, how he would smile to himself thinking nobody saw him when I told him that I was meeting up with Elliot, how he would ask me how Jorge's mother was doing and then later "accidentally" put too much money in my bank account for the month. I had spent my life looking for someone to love me loudly, but Dad loved me quietly as much as he could underneath my mother's reign. And as much as I want to hate him, I can't. Any difference, any disagreement that we had ever had was overshadowed by the one thing we had in common: both of us were victims of my mother, a simple, horrible reality that will bind us together forever.

"Your mother isn't well," Dad said for the second time that afternoon. He turned back to face me. "I'm not talking about her body. I'm talking about her head." His eyes, the same color as my own, grew stormy and angry. "It took me far, far too long to realize just how unwell she is, far too long to realize that she never really *wanted* an actual baby. All she wanted was to have a life that looked perfect and complete to anyone on the outside looking in. Infertility didn't fit in with that perfect little vision. I don't…I don't think she ever thought of a baby as a human being. It was something she wanted to keep like a trophy, just so she could *say* she had it, that she had given birth and she could check the experience off her 'things that perfect women do' list. And one baby wasn't enough. No. She wanted *more* even though she barely took care of the one she already had. So more trying. More miscarriages. More pregnancies that filled her with the false hope that she would someday end up with more babies even though she never really wanted them in the first place. And I'm sorry, Mia. I'm sorry I didn't see it all sooner. I was young and in love and stupid, and I'm just so sorry she didn't want you. No child deserves to be unwanted."

I shook my head. "I wasn't unwanted," I said resolutely. "I wasn't, Dad. Because *you* wanted me. Didn't you, Dad? You wanted me."

"Oh god, yes. You were my everything."

"But you never really showed it, did you, Dad?" My voice trembled with hurt. "You loved Mom too much. You picked her over me. You always picked her over me."

I expected him to cry, to protest, to shrivel up like the poor spineless creature he was. But he hit me with something completely unexpected instead.

"I left your mother."

He stood tall, resolute, unmoving, hands clasped in front of him. And amidst all the pain and sadness and remorse in his face, a little smirk played around the corners of his lips. "That's right," he said when I didn't reply. "I left her." And then he grew pensive and said, "Thirty years. Thirty years with your mother. Thirty years I'll never get back." And then his face turned red, and he looked at me in horror after realizing the magnitude of what he had just said.

But I felt no anger, no bitterness. Instead, I felt a warmth spread across my whole body. "Oh, Dad," I replied, and I began to sob, and he began to sob with me, and he came over and we embraced, and he smelled like Dad. My Dad. I had missed his smell so much. And oh, he was sad, so incredibly sad. What could I do? What could I say? I had the strongest urge to shield him from the world even though he was the one who should have always been shielding me.

"Do you believe in God?" I found myself whispering into his ear between sobs. He didn't answer me. "Well, I do," I lied. "God took thirty years from me, Dad. We both lost thirty years, you and me. But I'm not angry. Not anymore. I think God did it on purpose. He took thirty years from me because he knew you would need them. He's gonna give them to you. You're gonna get your thirty years back, Dad. These next thirty years, you're going to meet someone and fall in love, and she's going to give you the most beautiful babies, and the only thing I ask is that you tell them all about their big sister, Mia. Tell them that she's watching out for them. Will you do that?"

Dad just nodded into my shoulder as I blabbered on and on. The air was heavy with emotion, but I didn't want to let it go yet. "Can you do me a favor, Dad? Can you just keep telling me you love me? Just keep saying it. Please? Can I hear the words over and over again?"

So that's what happened. Maybe for an hour, maybe for three hours, I don't know. He just held me and stroked my hair and let me cry, and every few seconds, he would whisper that he loved me.

And every now and then, I would whisper back, "I love you too."

—Mia

November 22, 2089
Day 84, year 12

Yesterday was wild. I don't know if Dad really came to visit me or if it was all in my head. Jonah and Rose told me it really happened. But maybe, I imagined them telling me that. I can't trust anything I see or hear anymore. Not after what happened today. I know for a fact that what I saw today didn't really happen.

At eleven in the morning, I woke up to the sound of someone pounding on my door, and I was so startled that I jumped out of bed and onto my feet on the floor. That was the first sign that I was imagining it all. I haven't been out of my bed in three days. I'm too weak to stand, and I'm hooked up to Rose's constant stream of drugs.

But this morning, I wasn't attached to anything. My feet hit the floor, and I just walked right over to the door, and for some reason, it didn't seem strange at the time. The pounding on the door grew more and more relentless until I opened it, and that was the second sign that none of it was real.

It was Joel.

"Hello, Mia."

So familiar. So soothing. I had missed his voice so much. Involuntarily, I walked into him, and he put his arms around me, and he was strong and solid and everything that he was when I had met him on the shuttle for the very first time.

"God, I've missed you," he whispered into my hair. Then he pulled away and looked into my face. "You look so beautiful." And that was the third sign that none of it was real because I looked like a drugged-up old sick person. Even to Joel, who had seen me on my worst days, I couldn't have possibly been beautiful. But then, I looked over to my dresser, and I caught a glimpse of my face in the mirror.

It was my old face, or I guess I should say my *young* face, staring back at me. I was sixteen again. My hair looked like it did when I was having a good hair day, thick and wavy instead of dry and frizzy. My skin was smooth and pink, and when I smiled there were no wrinkles around my eyes and mouth.

"Hello, Mia," I echoed Joel's first greeting to my reflection.

I looked back at him. His face seemed younger too, almost like the face he had drawn in his self-portrait but not quite the same. Then I realized that it was *changing*, right before my eyes. He was aging backward. *Time* was aging backward, erasing our cancer, our mistakes, our fights, our deaths. None of it ever happened. We were Mia and Joel. We were young. We were meeting for the very first time.

I kissed him with my sixteen-year-old lips, and he kissed me back with his nineteen-year-old ones, and it was so wondrously awkward, like all teenage kissing is, when the power of your hormones and the depth of your experience are nowhere near the same but you just go for it anyway.

Sixteen! You are so precious and wonderful and enchanting, sixteen. I never appreciated you when I was you. I was always counting down days, looking ahead, always impatient for the next chapter of life to start and never stopping to immerse myself in the chapter I was still in. Don't do that, readers. You're going to miss out on so much.

Joel and I eventually separated, our hair and clothes not quite as in place as they were before. "Why are you here?" were the first words I uttered to him.

He smiled. "Am I supposed to be dead?" he asked.

"Well...*yeah*."

"Oh, that's right, I remember. You gave me drugs and killed me." He laughed.

I punched him in the arm in a way that was supposed to be playful, but my sixteen-year-old, cancer-free arm packed a lot more power than I had expected. His eyes widened. "Ouch! Damn, girl!"

And for some reason, being called "girl" while I was inhabiting a sixteen-year-old body was more arousing than being called "girl" while I was inhabiting a forty-seven-year-old body. The teenage hormones took over once more. We ended up on my bed, again engaging in the wonderful awkwardness that is teenage sexuality. Inexperience doesn't really matter when your body is young and flexible and your breasts are still perky and you don't have stretch marks to feel self-conscious about. And you're too focused on what you're doing to blurt out anything that you think sounds sexy in your head but will inevitably kill the mood if you say it out loud. And it's always over too quickly, but it doesn't matter because you're always up for giving it another go.

He wasn't really there. Neither was I. I knew that even while it was happening. But does it really matter? Sometimes, the most profound experiences we have are the ones that happen in our own heads.

"How do you feel?" Joel eventually asked me, and I knew he wasn't referring to the sex.

I answered him with the truth: "I'm afraid."

I'm afraid. Not of dying. I don't think it will hurt. I can barely feel anything anymore. I'm afraid of what comes after. I'm afraid of meeting God. But I'm even more afraid of meeting nothing at all.

"What happens, Joel? Where do we go?" I asked desperately.

He just smiled and shook his head. "No spoilers," he said.

I grabbed him by the shoulders. "Please," I begged him. "Please, tell me. I need to know what happens."

And then his smile faded, and he looked very sad and wise. He gently stroked my chin with his thumb and replied, "It's different for everyone. But there's nothing to be afraid of."

"But there's *something*, right? There's something after?"

"Of course there is. People don't just end."

And I felt a peace and relief that I can't even describe as I realized what my deepest fear had always been. "That's what I was scared of the most," I said. "I'm not scared of dying. I'm scared of ending."

He smiled again. "No. You won't end. You'll go on somewhere. We all do." Slowly, his body began to disappear in front of me, and I desperately tried to cling to it. He gently pushed my hands away.

"You don't have to do that," he said. "I told you. None of us end. I'm just going back to where I came from, that's all." He planted one last kiss on my forehead with transparent lips. "Just promise me you'll find me when you get there."

"I promise," I said. And he was gone.

—Mia

November 23, 2089
Day 85, year 12

Two days ago, I saw my dad, and I thought that was weird.

Yesterday, I saw a very much alive Joel, and I thought that was even weirder.

I don't think I'll be seeing anyone else after today. I'm too tired. My brain feels like a basketball that's been bouncing for a while and is just trying to roll and settle to a full stop. But if what I saw today really is the last thing I ever see, then I can die happy.

There were no knocks at the door. There were no sudden jolts out of bed. There was no shock. I opened my eyes this morning and somehow saw exactly what I've been expecting to see for the past year.

Four faces. Four smiles. Four sets of arms all holding onto each other's shoulders. Four hands that slowly and simultaneously stretched out to take mine. I don't know whose hand I grabbed. It doesn't matter. They pulled me straight up out of my bed, out of my room, out of the apartment, and we sat in a circle on the sand.

Juniper was the one who broke the silence first. "Truth or dare?" she asked me with a smile. The boys all smiled too as they sat awaiting my answer. And even though I had always been a "truther," this game felt different.

"Dare," I answered.

The beach disappeared. The boys disappeared. Suddenly, it was just Juniper and me standing at the foot of my bed. My old, sick body was still lying there motionless. Juniper walked over to it and rested her hand on top of its sleeping head. "I dare you to forgive yourself," she said.

I felt my throat tighten. "For what?" I asked.

"You know for what."

I did. I did know for what.

I could have told someone about her dad. I could have helped her get away. I could have protected her sisters. She had told me not to tell. I shouldn't have listened.

"I dare you to forgive yourself," she said again.

Her past dares had almost always involved doing something naked. Somehow, this dare felt even more exposing. I started crying.

"I'm so sorry about the girls," I stammered out between sobs. "I'm sorry I never told anyone."

But Juniper just smiled really big at me and wrapped me up in her strong arms. "The girls are fine!" she excitedly reassured me. "They're fine! I'm watching over them. He hasn't touched them. Not once!"

I pulled away, awestruck. "Really?"

She laughed. "Yeah. I go down and visit the bastard from time to time. I'll just stand there at the foot of his bed, and he wakes up all freaked out, and then when he screams for my mom, I disappear before she wakes up. She thinks he's crazy!" She laughed even harder. "I'm *haunting* him, Mia! He knows what he did. He'll never tell anyone about it. But he won't go near those girls."

And the image of Juniper's dad pissing his pants in fear of her ghostly form was so damn funny that I started laughing right along with her, and as we laughed, we were pulled back onto the beach, back into the circle, back into the rest of the game. Juniper sat next to Matty. She turned to him and grazed his hand with hers in a way that made it impossible to tell if she had done it on purpose or not.

"Your turn," she said to him playfully, and he looked down at their hands and blushed. Even in the afterlife, those two are so in love it's ridiculous.

Matty looked up at me. "Truth or dare?" he asked me.

And once again, I replied with "Dare."

And once again, the beach and the others disappeared, and I was back in my room, this time with Matty. He stood next to my nightstand where my journal rested. Slowly, he picked it up, stroked its spine, and gently flipped through the pages. Still a gentle giant. He wiped tears from his eyes.

"I dare you to believe in yourself," he said as he pressed the journal into my chest.

I took it from him. It had been a while since I had read anything in it. Nearly every page is full now. Full of words. Full of poems. Full of me.

"Believe in this," Matty insisted. "Believe that after you're gone, it's going to change someone's life." He wrapped his arms around me, sandwiching the journal between us. "You did it, Mia. You became a writer. Just like we always talked about. Do you believe me?"

"Yes" was my muffled reply as I pressed my face into his torso. I had missed Matty's hugs. And in that moment, it was true. I believed in Matty. I believed in me.

Back on the beach, still in Matty's arms, I felt another hand on my shoulder. I turned to see Jorge's classic light-up-the-room smile.

"Truth or dare, Mia?" He grabbed my hand and pulled me toward him. And before the word "dare" was completely out of my mouth, we were in my room.

My body was still in the bed. My journal was still on the night-stand. But Jorge's attention was on my only other worldly possession in the room, the drawing that Joel had made for me. He picked it up, mesmerized.

"This is incredible," he said. "Where did you get it?"

I felt a jab in my heart, a fist around my insides that held me back, a voice that whispered "No." No. My life had been split in two neat pieces, the "before" and the "now." No. Don't let them mix. Joel doesn't belong in the "before." Jorge doesn't belong in the "now."

"A friend gave it to me," I finally answered.

Jorge didn't respond. His gaze alternated between my young face in the picture and my old face asleep on the pillow. I knew his mind was full of things to say. I also knew that he wouldn't say any of them until he had thought of the exact right words to use. He came close to me and stood with his toes almost touching mine. He lifted my chin gently with one hand and held up the picture next to my face with the other.

"Do you miss yourself?" he finally asked me. "Do you miss this person that I'm holding in my hands?" His big, dark eyes held nothing back. Tears began pouring out of them while mine stayed dry as I considered the question.

Did I miss myself?

But wasn't I still the same person in a different body?

What was it that I was really missing? What was my heart aching for?

"I don't care about myself at all," I answered resolutely. "I miss *you*. I miss all of you. I'd trade myself in for any of you, and I wouldn't think twice."

"Why?" Jorge asked. He continued to hold my chin up and wouldn't let me look away. "Why do you feel that way?"

I let my eyes unfocus until his face was nothing but a swirl of brown shades. "You deserve to be here. I don't," I answered simply.

He shook his head as he finally released me. He looked upset, angry even. Violently, he spun around, letting me stare at the back of his head. "I picked 'dare,'" I said. "You can't ask me these things. You have to give me a dare."

"This isn't about the game!" Jorge shouted at the wall.

"Well, we're still playing. And I picked 'dare.'" I stayed calm. He wasn't getting off the hook. "Did you hear me? I said I picked 'dare'!"

Suddenly, he collapsed in front of me, and I jumped back. We weren't in my room anymore. We were in the alley behind the dumpster. We were in the last place I had seen him, and he was crumpled on the ground in the same exact position as he had been that night. Then I felt the knife.

It hadn't hit anything important. I would be fine. I would be stitched up and bandaged and hauled off to a cell. It still hurt anyway. And I crumpled up and landed next to Jorge.

He wasn't moving. His eyes were open. They were still weeping. Blood dribbled from his mouth. There were shouts, there were sirens, but they were all muffled and quiet compared to the sound of my own heart pounding in my ears. I began to convulse in shock. I reached up a shaking hand to touch Jorge's cheek. It was cold.

"I picked 'dare,' Jorge," I whispered, and I slowly began to cry. "I picked 'dare'!"

The sirens still howled. The shouts still pierced the air, heavy with the smell of blood and garbage. Jorge still didn't move.

"I'm sorry, Jorge!" I sobbed. "I'm sorry! I'll play your way, Jorge. I'll play however you want. You can ask me anything, I swear! Please, Jorge!"

And then the sirens stopped, the shouting stopped, the pain and the blood and the pounding in my head stopped. Jorge blinked and let out a single, ragged breath. More blood trickled out from between his lips as they opened up, desperately trying to form words. The words were so quiet that I'm not sure if I actually heard them or if I just felt them in my heart, but I was sure of what they said.

"I dare you to love yourself. Love yourself like you love all of us."

And then I felt the soft sand under my body, and the air turned salty again and we were all safe, together. Jorge was sitting upright along with everyone else, no longer bleeding or crying or struggling to breathe. They all waited patiently for my response, looking at me with anticipation.

"I don't know how," I whispered.

"Try anyway," Jorge replied.

And they gathered around me and closed in until I felt nothing but the warmth of their arms holding onto me, lifting me, and then I felt it. I felt their love turn into mine. I felt them all become one with me, and when I opened my eyes, I couldn't see them anymore, but god, they were with me. And they've stayed with me ever since.

But there was still one more person that needed to play.

"Elliot?" I whispered into the darkness.

And a voice inside my head answered back, "I'm here."

I heard his voice. I felt his arms. I saw his green eyes. They were all in my head, but it's like I said before, sometimes the most profound experiences we have are the ones that happen inside our own heads.

"Don't cry, Mia," he said gently, and I felt the wetness around my eyes begin to dry up, leaving only a tingling warmth. He said it again, "Don't cry, Mia," and he said it a few more times until all my tears were gone. And then for the last time, I heard the question, "Truth or dare?"

It had been so easy with the others. The word "dare" had escaped my lips before I even had time to think about it. With Elliot, it was different. I wasn't sure at first how to answer. I had already been dared to forgive myself, to believe in myself, to love myself. What was left for him to dare me to do? On the other hand, answering "truth" seemed so stupid. Elliot knew everything about me. I had never held anything back from him. But then I felt my heart being pulled, and in the tiniest, most innocuous voice, I heard the phrase, "He still needs to know something."

"Truth," I breathed out.

I think maybe I'd had my eyes closed until then or I was so deep in my own head that I couldn't actually see anything. Either way, Elliot's form finally began to take shape in front of me, and he was beautiful and familiar and perfect, and then I realized that we were both naked, but there wasn't anything sexual about it. It's hard to explain. I guess it must have been what Adam and Eve felt like in the garden of Eden.

"Okay," I heard his voice, and this time, I heard it outside of my own head coming from his mouth. It felt like hearing a favorite song that you hadn't heard in years, and yet the moment it begins to play, you instantly know every word, every chord, every cadence. It felt like comfort. It felt like home.

"Tell me," he said, "tell me exactly how you feel about me."

I looked at him in disbelief for a second. "What?" I asked.

He repeated himself, "Tell me exactly how you feel about me."

I didn't know what was more ridiculous, the question or the fact that I actually didn't know how to answer. And with every silent second that passed, I began to feel more and more afraid.

How did I feel about Elliot? How could I even put it into words? Where could I even *start*?

"Just say it. Say anything," he urged me. And I thought that maybe if I just started talking, eventually, the right words would come out.

"Well, I miss you," I began. Damn. I couldn't even make it four words without the tears starting again. "I miss you every day. I love you. I think about you all the time. I don't know if I ever believed you were actually gone. But I still feel this emptiness, and I think you're the only person who can fill it." And then the words began to come faster, and I stumbled over them. "But I also met someone else. And I loved him too. And he made me so, so happy for a little while, and he made the emptiness not feel quite so…*empty*. And I had to choose between feeling empty and not feeling empty. And I chose to not feel empty even though I knew it wasn't fair. I broke the rules. Choosing to love someone means that you get to feel pure ecstasy for a little bit of time and then complete agony for the rest of it. And that was a trade I was too scared to make. So I stopped loving you and started loving someone else because the agony was too much for me. And do you know what happened? He left. And I felt the agony all over again. I gave you up just to feel happy again, and in the end, it didn't even work."

I gasped as the weight of it all escaped my chest. Was that it? Was that the truth, and had I not realized it before? But Elliot just shook his head and smiled. He took a step toward me, leaned forward, and whispered into my ear, "Liar."

"What do you mean, 'liar'?"

"Come on, Mia. That was all bullshit, and you know it."

"No, it wasn't! I cheated. I didn't play fair."

And then he laughed and said, "That's not even *possible*. What you're describing isn't a real *thing*."

I tried to look away, but he wouldn't let me. He cupped my face in his hands, touching me for the first time since the day he died, and then he kissed me.

"What was his name?" he asked while his lips still grazed mine. I hesitated. He reassured. "It's okay. Tell me his name."

"Joel," I managed to answer.

"Do you love him?"

"Yes."

"Do you love me?"

"Yes."

And slowly, we pulled apart, and he smiled again and winked. "See? Was that so hard to say?"

I started sobbing again. "I'm sorry," I choked out.

"For what?"

"For loving someone else."

"Why are you sorry for that?"

"Because love doesn't count if you run from the pain of it and toward something else."

"No. You're wrong," and he grew more insistent as he spoke. "That's not what love is. It's not a game. There's no 'counting.' Do you really think it matters if you love one person or two people or ten people? Do you think a mother loves her first kid less after she has a second one? Love isn't this finite resource that we can only give to one person. It doesn't get thinner when you spread it around. That's not how love *works*, Mia." And then he said the words I had heard before but hadn't really believed yet, "Love doesn't take up space, it doesn't crowd, it doesn't push anything out. It does the opposite. It makes your heart bigger and bigger—"

"Until you can fit the whole world inside of it," I finished.

It's been a few hours since that encounter on the beach. I can't stop thinking about it though. They all knew. They knew me so well. Everything I needed summed up into three words: forgiveness, belief, love. Joel was right. None of us ever "end." I'll find him, and then I'll find Juniper and Matty and Jorge and Elliot. And I will love them all. And there will be others too. I will find the people who need me, or maybe, they will find me first, and I will love them. There is enough of me for everyone.

Do you need someone to love you? You can find me. I don't know where I'll be, so I'm sorry I can't give you better directions. But by now, you know me pretty well. Maybe, you'll know where to look.

—Mia

November 25, 2089
Day 87, year 12

Talking is getting harder and harder to do. Rose understands. She just sits with me and keeps me company. She's moved two chairs next to my bed. One is for her. The other is for Jonah. They'll both be here when it happens. It won't be long now, maybe just a few more days. So I wanted to say thank you, just in case this is my last entry. Thank you for reading my story. I want you to not feel sorry or sad for me. I just want you to take every advantage you can of your own life. Do good things. Love recklessly. Tell your truth to the world. I don't have anything else to say. I'm an old person who hasn't lived long enough to glean very much wisdom. But I got a whole year of life that I was able to live in this body, and that was a blessing I didn't deserve. I got to fall in love again. I got to see my face, my real face. I got to watch all of the seasons change one last time. I'm at peace. I hope you are too. And I hope that I'm there if you ever need me. I promise I'll do my best.

—Mia

Dear Reader,

My name is Rose Burke. I was Mia's nurse. Last night, on November 27, 2089, Mia passed away peacefully in her sleep. She was seventeen years old.

This afternoon, she will be cremated, and her family will be notified of her death. They will have thirty days to claim her ashes. If they are not claimed, then her friend, Jonah, and I will take them and scatter them around the oak tree outside the aging facility, which was one of her final wishes.

I haven't been a nurse very long. I graduated at the top of my class and became the youngest person in history to work in the aging labs. As a medical professional, I was fascinated and thrilled to be a part of such a groundbreaking new science. I expected every door to be flung wide open in my career. I could do whatever I wanted. What I did not expect, however, were my patients.

Contrary to popular belief, criminals are not one-sided people. They have families. They are artists, musicians, writers. Some are brilliant. Some seem to always be happy no matter what. One of my patients, right before he was sedated, handed me the most beautiful, intricate paper rose. "I used my napkin from dinner last night," he told me with a smile. "I spent hours trying to make the perfect flower. A rose for my Rose." And he chuckled and slowly closed his eyes and went to sleep. He was already quite old. He didn't survive his procedure. I took a leave of absence for a week after that and alternated between sleeping, crying, and staring blankly into space in my tiny bedroom. I still have that rose.

I'm not here to talk about me though. I'm not even here to talk about politics and what we can do to change them. I'm here to tell you the truth about Mia.

She was quiet. She only spoke when she needed to and never spoke to me about personal things. The only thing I knew for certain about her was that she always had her notebook nearby and never let anyone see what was inside. She died with it in her arms, held loosely; I took it as a sign that it was finally time for me to open it. I've spent all day reading it, only pausing when I need to cry.

Here are the things that you need to know about Mia. You need to know that Mia was a good person. Please, please, know that. And you need to know that she was beautiful. Truly beautiful. Her eyes shone behind her glasses, her skin glowed, her hair hung in silky gray waves that perfectly caressed her shoulders. But that didn't even matter in the end because her spirit is what made her truly beautiful.

Mia was right about what she said in the beginning. So many of us have kept track of the real date, real time, real ages. I think a lot of us are holding out hope that this is all temporary, a horrible experiment gone wrong, a calamity that will eventually disappear under a different government and exist only in the confines of history. And maybe, by the time you are reading this, all that will have come to pass. I hope to God it has.

After I make sure Mia's ashes are taken care of, I'm leaving the aging facility. I don't know what I'll do next. I just know I can't work there anymore. I can't bear to watch one more person's life taken away, to stare helplessly as an unconscious human being slowly turns gray and wrinkled as hundreds of chemicals are pumped through their body, to have to be the one to wake them up after weeks of putting them through hell and back and watching them break down as the horrible new reality sets in.

Don't worry about me though. Don't even think about me. This story isn't about me, not in the slightest. I want you all, whoever you may be, to simply keep Mia alive. Tell her story to anyone who will listen. Think of her happy and reunited with her loves. Mourn the years she lost and vow that you will not waste a single second of the life you've been given.

I think I'll leave you with the last thing Mia said to me after I asked her if she had any last words. She was too weak to speak, but she motioned for a pen and paper and slowly, painstakingly wrote out her final words. It took about ten minutes for her to write out a few sentences, and she had to pause after every word, but eventually, she finished it and looked up at me with the loveliest smile I had ever seen. We shared silent tears together, and I gently took her frail, cold hand in mine. I put her note in my pocket, determined not to read it until she was gone. This is what it said:

> *To anyone who has made a mistake, a terrible, terrible mistake, you are more than the worst thing you ever did. Your life means something. Figure out what it is and don't waste it.*

—Mia

The End

ABOUT THE AUTHOR

Marissa Dike is a musician, composer, and writer currently residing in Ohio with her husband, two daughters, and two cats that enjoy licking the butter off her toast every morning. To find out more about her books, writing projects, and music, visit WritingMarissa. com or find her on Facebook at www.facebook.com/marissadike. She can also be found on Instagram and Twitter through the handle @ writingmarissa.

CPSIA information can be obtained
at www.ICGtesting.com
Printed in the USA
BVHW071447090222
628492BV00006B/451